Breaking All the Rules

Also by Cynthia Sax

Flashes of Me
The Seen Trilogy:
He Claims Me
He Touches Me
He Watches Me

Breaking All the Rules

An Erotic Novella

CYNTHIA SAX

AVON
IMPULSE

An Imprint of HarperCollins Publishers

Excerpt from *Flashes of Me* copyright © 2014 by Cynthia Sax.

EPub Edition APRIL 2014 ISBN: 9780062328212

Print Edition ISBN: 9780062328236

JV 10 9 8 7 6 5 4 3 2 1

Chapter One

THIS IS THE morning I break Nathan Lawford, Blaine Technologies' notoriously uptight chief financial officer, the executive employees call the Iceman.

I hum the words to an extremely vulgar hip-hop song as I stride through the concrete-and-glass lobby, my phone in my right hand and the straps of my backpack slung over my shoulder.

Not even Jerome, the company's powerful high-security guard, could dampen my enthusiasm today. He searched my black canvas bag for a record twelve minutes, wrinkling important papers and poking his clumsy fingers into delicate electronics. He leered and sneered at me, and I said nothing, tolerating the harassment.

Because today Nate will touch me.

I've spent months defrosting the Iceman, following rules I've crafted, rules he isn't aware of. I can't touch him unless he touches me. I can't see him outside of our morning elevator rides unless he approaches me. I can e-mail him but not call him, check his agenda but not change it.

Even with these self-imposed restrictions, I'll win, my victory growing more certain as our daily skirmishes escalate in intensity.

Every morning Nate takes the same elevator at the same time, his schedule as rigid and unbending as he is. Every morning I share the same elevator car. He looks at me. I look at him. We exchange a couple of verbal barbs, some increasingly steamy sexual innuendos, and then we part ways, going to our different floors, our different worlds.

I'm the green-haired rebel intern. Nate is an unemotional rule setter, a huge immovable wall I can't stop pushing against, a challenge I can't back away from. He drives me absolutely wild and I will have him. On my terms.

I glance at my phone's screen. Shit on a stick. I have three minutes to trek to the elevators. Clipping my phone to my skirt's frayed waistband, I march faster, the heels of my shoes ringing against the gleaming white marble tile. Video screens hang from the walls, displaying happy images of the conforming masses. Dark-suited corporate clones linger around the paid-to-be-perky receptionist.

Loitering isn't an option, as there's no flexibility in the Iceman's timetable. I turn the corner and my heels squeak on the floor. No one is waiting for the elevators, the area empty. I press the up button three times in rapid succession, pleased that I'll have Nate's complete attention during our five-minute elevator ride.

Privacy is essential for my plan to work, as I'm not the type of woman any career-minded executive would choose to acknowledge publicly. I glance at my reflection in the elevator's shiny metallic doors and wince. Although I no longer wear my temporary tattoos or visible body jewelry, the green hair and the holes in my ears, nose, and bottom lip remain, declaring my rebel status to the world.

This is who I am, who I've always been. I break rules. I push people. I don't fit in anywhere. I tell myself I'm okay with this. In my heart I know I'm not. But I can't change, not even for the Iceman.

The bell rings, the doors to elevator number four open, and my heart pounds. Nate stands in the back right corner, staring down at his phone, appearing as unapproachably handsome as usual, his blond hair short and neat, his broad shoulders clad in a form-fitting black suit, his crisp white shirt accentuating his golden tan. His tie is always black, always plain.

He wears the same clothing combination every day, and I want to peel the monochromatic fabric away from his kicking hot physique and lick him from his head to his toes. This impulsive act, while certain to be sexually satisfying, violates the rules of my game. He must touch me first. I keep my hands to myself and stride into the elevator, my hips swaying and my head held defiantly high.

Nate glances upward, our gazes lock and hold, and I forget to breathe, to think, to move. His eyes are the palest, coldest gray, a frigid blast of icy wind on a hot Californian day, and I want him as I've never wanted anyone else, my need for him carnal and raw.

He slides his phone into his jacket pocket and the silver Rolex on his wrist gleams. This symbol of wealth and the establishment, a physical reminder of who Nate is, doesn't squelch my lust. It perversely feeds my fantasies.

In my overactive imagination Nate doesn't stay in his corner. He stalks toward me, hooks one of his arms around my waist, pulls my curves into his muscle, and—

"Miss Trent." His crisp businesslike tone returns me to reality.

"Nate." I mimic his curtness, breaking an unspoken company rule by addressing a top executive by his first name. I tap the button for the legal floor. This is the law-enforcing, super-quiet department I've been sentenced to. I don't fit in there, but then, I've never fit in anywhere.

Except here. I belong in this elevator car. I belong with Nate. I claim the corner across from him and openly study the object of my obsession. "You spent another weekend alone, I see." The lines around his mouth and eyes are deeply etched, attesting to his many months of celibacy. This pleases me. I don't want Nate to touch any other woman. He's my iceberg to melt.

He raises one of his eyebrows. "Have you added stalking to your long list of crimes?"

I roll my eyes. I was found guilty of three minor misdemeanors while I was a careless teenager and now I've been labeled a criminal for life. "Don't flatter yourself. A blind woman can tell you're not getting any." I stretch the truth. His expression is as cold and as emotionless as it normally is.

Nate frowns, glances at his reflection in the mirrored walls, sweeps one of his hands over his perfect hair.

"What's the matter?" I grin at him as I set my backpack on the floor by my feet. "Are all of the hookers in LA on strike?"

He returns his gaze to me and narrows his eyes. "You're well informed." Ice drips from his words, his coolness indicating I've scored a direct hit. Many people subjected to Nate's subzero demeanor assume he's a frigid, unfeeling bastard. I recognize it for what it is—a shield, as effective as my sarcasm and green hair.

"You bet I'm well informed." It didn't take me long to discover that every well-dressed, insanely beautiful woman appearing beside Nate in the newspaper's society pages was a high-end escort. His hooker fetish doesn't bother me. Nate is a faithful, serial-monogamous John, taking a long time to choose the right escort and then paying for her exclusive attentions.

"You're not hideous." I unbutton my formerly black blazer, the sole suit I own faded from having been hand washed every night. "Why do you pay for sex?"

"Everyone pays for sex in one way or another." Nate visually tracks my movements as I shrug out of the garment, removing one more barrier between us. "Some muddle the price with talk of love and feelings. I prefer straightforward, honest negotiations."

He prefers to live life on his terms, laws be damned. I find this sexy, very sexy. I roll back my shoulders, my muscles tight from having carried the backpack, my movements deliberately sensuous.

Nate's gaze lowers to the pale curves threatening to spill out of my favorite black leather corset. He peruses my breasts thoroughly, leisurely, his eyes darkening to a stormy gray. An exciting awareness radiates from him, causing my nipples to pucker and my body to hum.

"What are you doing, Miss Trent?" His voice is low and tongue-suckingly deep, making me think of entwined limbs and tangled bedsheets.

"I'm hot." I drift my fingertips across my cleavage, teasing my skin, tormenting him, the man I must and will have. "And I'm moist. Do you have a tissue?"

Nate hesitates before extracting a neatly folded square of pristine white fabric from the inside pocket of his jacket. He holds it out to me.

I reach for the handkerchief, my fingers brush against his, and a sensual spark surges up my arm, lighting fires throughout my body. Nate's mask of ice slips for two heartbeats, revealing a hunger as raw and as savage as my own. He then yanks his hand away, and this hunger is concealed, sealed by a layer of frost.

He wants me. Badly. I pat the sinfully soft cotton over my breasts, and Nate's clean, fresh-out-of-the-shower scent transfers from the fabric onto my skin. He watches me, his expression carefully blank. Only his eyes convey his emotions, his gaze dark and intense.

"You need to get laid, Nate," I bluntly state, hoping to shock him into action, to snap his control as he's snapping mine.

Nate leans closer, looming over me, tall and overpoweringly masculine. "Are you making me an offer, Miss

Trent?" His body heat weaves seductively around my chest, over my stomach, between my thighs.

"Would you be interested if I was?" I tilt my chin defiantly upward, bringing my lips nearer to his. "I'm not one of your vanilla sex yes-women." I skim his handkerchief over my black corset, polishing the leather with the cotton square. "Do you think you can handle me, big boy?"

My challenge is a bluff. I doubt I can handle him. I haven't had sex in over two years, all of my excess time and energy spent on the charity website and app I'm designing.

"I can handle you." Nate's voice deepens even more, his husky tones curling my toes. He meets my gaze, holding it.

In his eyes I see the temptation of locked doors and the lure of deep dark secrets, both of these impossible for me to resist. I lean forward, balancing on my toes, and Nate lowers his grim mouth until his lips are a lick away from mine. As he breathes out I breathe in, every inch of me conscious of every inch of him.

"But I won't accept your challenge, Miss Trent, tempting though it might be." He pulls away from me and the passion between us dissipates, evaporating into the cool air. "I only deal with professionals. I give them cash. They give me sex. There are no disappointments, no unreasonable expectations, no promises of love or forever."

This is the second time he's mentioned love. "I didn't ask you for love or forever, Romeo." I know who I am. I'm the girl a college boy screws in a back alley after a rave. I'm not the woman any man brings home to his parents.

"You didn't have to ask me for love." Nate watches me warily, his spine rigidly straight and his shoulders squared. "You grew up on a hippie commune. Peace and love are what you believe in."

I jerk my chin upward, surprised he knows where I grew up. My past isn't something I talk about. "You forgot freedom," I point out. "Peace, love, and freedom are what hippies believe in." I didn't follow my parents' all-natural path, being too fascinated with technology and other modern conveniences, but I do believe in those three ideals.

"Yes, freedom. You believe everything should be free," Nate says. "Including information that should remain private." His voice is edged with disapproval. "You don't have any desire for money."

He's correct. I don't have any desire for money. I do, however, desire him. Too much. If he asked me, I'd drop to my knees, unzip his black dress pants, and suck him dry right here, right now, in the corporate elevator, uncaring of the security cameras, of our coworkers, of my rules.

"Put your blazer back on, Miss Trent." Nate slams the brakes on my sexual fantasy. "I'm not interested." His gaze flicks to my breasts.

"Bullshit." I ball up the handkerchief and whip it at him. Nate catches the fabric and nonchalantly stuffs the handkerchief into the right pocket of his pants, his control infuriating me.

"You're very interested." I thrust my arms into the sleeves of the blazer and yank the garment closed. "Right now you're wondering if my breasts are as full, as soft as they appear." His eyes flash a warning I can't and won't heed, my pride smarting from his rejection. "You're asking yourself how I taste, if I'm wet, hot, tight."

The elevator doors open and I don't move. I stare at Nate, huffing with indignation and sexual frustration. I want him and I know he wants me. Why won't he touch me?

"This is your floor, Miss Trent." Nate's voice drips ice. His response should cool me down. It doesn't. It heats me up, pushing me to the point of combustion.

"The answer is yes. I *am* wet, hot, tight." I grab my backpack. "I'm all of that and more." I stomp out of the elevator. "And Nate?" I glance over my shoulder and meet his glacier gaze. "I taste delicious." The doors close between us.

He'll be thinking about me all day. I strut down the hallway, my head held high, a jaunty bounce to my walk.

The office walls are painted gray. The industrial carpet and cubicle dividers are a shade darker. My coworkers are dressed in black and white, their suits crisp and their hair neat.

I call out cheery good-mornings as I pass people. A prissy woman with carefully arranged blond curls shushes me. A grim-looking woman clucks her tongue. Silence is the unspoken rule on the legal floor.

I don't follow other people's silly rules and wish the next coworker I meet a louder good-morning. My dad says I can't help myself. I'm the evolution of the hippie, the offspring of two rebellious souls, genetically inclined for anarchy, taught to question everything.

All I know is I don't fit in. Anywhere. I left the commune because the members wanted to restrict my computer time, their weak-assed attempt to convert me failing. I got booted out of the hacking community because I pushed too hard for peace and love. I certainly don't belong here, at Blaine Technologies.

I venture deeper into corporate America. The sea of gray is constant and never ending. The lights are fluorescent. The hum of printers softens the quiet. Somewhere Mother Earth is weeping.

"Green," Miss Yen, my boss, hollers, the tiny lawyer always knowing when I arrive. I hurry into her office, rapping my knuckles against the door as I enter.

My stylish boss clearly had no input in decorating her office. Ugly vertical blinds cover the floor-to-ceiling windows. An even uglier modern painting hangs on one interior wall, meaningless stripes of white and gray slashing a stark black canvas.

Filing cabinets line the perimeter, forming a wall of temptation I couldn't resist. Their flimsy locks were no match for me. I scanned the contents one late night and found nothing of interest, Miss Yen keeping her secrets elsewhere.

She stands behind her black lacquer desk, her hands on her hips, a scowl on her beautiful face. Her dark suit hugs her slim body. A long silver scar skims across one of her cheeks. Gray file folders stuffed with paper are stacked on the desk in front of her.

My shoulders slump. I recognize these files, having spent six endless days compiling them. "Is there a problem with the expense reports?"

"Is there a problem?" The woman known as the dragon lady snorts. "You might say that. Finance rejected them."

The finance department is Nate's realm, staffed with employees as uptight and unbending as he is. "They rejected *all* of the expense reports?"

"All of them," Miss Yen confirms. "If finance finds an error in one report, their new policy is to reject the entire submission." Her lips twist. "Supposedly they're busy with security issues." She glances at me. "You wouldn't know anything about that, would you, Green?"

"Why would I know anything about that?" I strive to appear as innocent as I possibly can. If Nate had correctly named me as the culprit, Mr. Henley, Blaine Technologies' head of cybersecurity, would have already fired me. He warned me that my next violation would be my last. It seems the company caps allowable employee offenses at thirty-two.

"Leave the other departments alone and focus on this task." Miss Yen pushes the stack of files toward me. "Confirm each and every line. Once Mr. Lawford sets rules he doesn't deviate from them. If the expense reports have errors he *will* reject them again."

"Yes, Miss Yen." Nate's sexual frustration is causing trouble for everyone, and I should feel contrite. What I feel is smug satisfaction. His control is severely compromised, my victory over him imminent. I haul the files back to my gray cubicle.

No one else sits in temp row. Kat, my friend and fellow intern, has been promoted. She's spending all of her personal time planning her fashionista wedding to

Mr. Henley. Anna, another best friend, is a new mom and works for her husband, Gabriel Blaine, the CEO and founder of Blaine Technologies. Both women are head over heels in love with their executives.

I have nothing except a sure-to-be short-lived sexapalooza with an Iceman and a charitable side project I don't know how to launch. The pinch-faced lady seated one row over fills the air with floral-scented fumes. I add one crazy work neighbor to my list.

I toss my backpack into an empty desk drawer, log onto my computer, and peruse the first expense report, confirming line after line. The coding is correct. The numbers tie back to the receipts. The only mistake I find is a two-cent variance on one of the totals, a freakish error due to exchange rates and rounding.

Blaine Technologies is a billion-dollar company and the expense reports have been rejected for a two-cent discrepancy. I grin. Nate will be mine before the end of the week.

I tap on the keyboard and access his schedule. The security issues that have him concerned don't include his account. His password, MoneyMan7, remains the same. I add "Think about Camille's breasts" to his to-do list.

Mere minutes pass before he checks this line item as completed. Nathan Lawford is thinking about my breasts. This lifts my spirits and I hum happily as I examine the next expense report.

Is he stroking himself while he fantasizes about me? Has he closed his office door, unzipped his pants, and curled his fingers around his thick cock? His shaft will be as straight and as rigid as he is, the hair around his base blond, fine, and neatly trimmed.

I shift in my chair, my pussy moistening. He'll pump himself vigorously, in sure up-and-down strokes, as unrelenting with his own body as he is with the expense reports. A dab of pre-cum will form on his tip. I lick my lips.

Will he taste as clean and as fresh as he smells? I've hacked into his medical records, the escort company he favors requiring regular checkups. Nate is healthy, virile, a male in his prime.

And he's thinking of me, quirky, crazy Camille Trent. I unclip my phone from my waistband, open my blazer, and take a photo of my breasts. The black corset I'm wearing contrasts vividly with my ivory skin and the overhead lights deepen the shadow between my curves, making me appear even better endowed than I already am. I send this naughty image to Nate's personal e-mail account, giving him more to think about.

Teasing my sexually frustrated executive brightens my otherwise dull day. I smile and apply all of my attention to the stack of expense reports, determined to follow the rules for once in my insubordinate life and give Nate the perfection he requires.

Chapter Two

BY NOON THE numbers on the expense reports blur, the lines running together. I set the stack aside, remove my lunch from the backpack, and saunter to the break room. The space is empty, my coworkers preferring to buy food from the company-subsidized cafeteria.

The meals served there are good, but not as good as my beef panang curry, a recipe I learned from Auntie Ratana, one of my mom's best friends. I warm up the dish and carry it back to my desk, looking forward to enjoying this little taste of home.

The pinch-faced lady seated one row away from me complains loudly about stinky foods. She must be complaining about her own dish. She's eating steamed broccoli, and the scent of flatulence hangs heavily in the air.

I ignore her grumbling, open my data donation program, and eat slowly as I code, savoring the flavors of curry paste, coconut milk, lime, and basil.

The program I'm crafting is my gift to the world, a means of sharing unused data and voice capacity. The less fortunate often receive free used phones, but not the plans needed to utilize them. My program will fix that problem.

There's no money in it. When it goes live next year I might snag a Blaine Technologies' Change the World grant. The mentoring provided is direly needed. The funding, however, will only pay for additional business expenses, not for my rent or my grocery bill. Nate would call my project's lack of profit unsustainable.

I peruse his schedule. He has booked a lunchtime meeting with Mr. Blaine. My friend Anna's desk is situated outside of her enigmatic CEO's office, and I should drop by, see Emily, the adorable heir to the Blaine Technologies' empire. If I bump into Nate as he leaves his meeting, I can claim it's a coincidence.

It wouldn't truly be a coincidence and this would violate the rules of my game. Nate must choose to see me outside the confines of our morning elevator rides. I can't see him. I force myself to remain at my desk, to concentrate on my project, to not think about the object of my doomed and completely absurd obsession.

My progress is slow. Coding is natural for me. I've been taking programs apart and putting them back together since I was a child, computers being a necessary evil at the commune. Designing the site is more challenging. I stress over every marketing decision, every color choice, every graphic and text I utilize.

The small hairs on the back of my neck rise and my body hums with awareness. Only one man has this effect on me, but it can't be him. He has a meeting. I glance upward and my jaw drops.

It *is* him. Nate stands at the end of the row of empty cubicles, his expression blank, his back straight, and his feet braced apart. His fingers clench into fists and release, clench and release. He's the Iceman, renowned for his restraint, yet he's struggling with his control. This is how much he wants me.

"I thought you had a meeting with your boss." I issue this statement as a challenge. He'll know I checked his schedule, accessed his account.

"I canceled the meeting."

He canceled his meeting with Mr. Blaine. Nate never cancels meetings. His schedule once drafted is set for the day.

"Did you?" I ask.

"Yes." Nate's gaze meets mine and I suck in my breath. His pale gray eyes are turbulent with stark, raw emotion, his need calling to me, seducing me.

"I see." I stare at him. He stares back at me, his square jaw jutted and his lips pressed together. Tension radiates from him, heavy waves of desire dragging me down, down, down.

"Okie dokie, then," I concede. He came to me. He canceled his meeting for me. I can do the rest.

I push away from my desk and walk toward him, my hips swaying, my soul filled with purpose. Nate watches me, not moving, not speaking.

"Come with me." I cover his fists with my fingers. Energy surges from his hands to mine, the connection instant and intense, shaking my soul.

"Come," I repeat, leading him toward the shredding room, grabbing a box of tissues as we pass an unoccupied desk. Nate follows me, issuing no protests, offering no resistance.

I want resistance. I want push back, challenge, him. Nate's unbending personality is an integral part of him and I don't want him to change, not for me, not for anyone.

We enter the shredding room, the space soundproof, private, utilitarian. A monstrous machine is bookended by two stacks of folded cardboard boxes. Shelves line the perimeter. White dust hangs in the stale air and covers the gray frayed carpet.

"This isn't posh, but it will do." I set the box of tissues on a nearby shelf and close the door, blocking the outside noise and hiding us from curious eyes, creating a secluded office oasis for the two of us.

"We're not doing anything, Miss Trent." Nate stands dangerously close to the exit and watches me warily, prepared to leave at the slightest provocation. "I only deal with professionals." The erection tenting his black dress pants belies his words.

He wants me, needs me, yet he fights me, his continued resistance presenting a challenge I'm driven to accept. "I can please you as well as any professional can." I lean into him and cover his impressively large cock with my hands, feeling the length and width of him through the fabric.

He jerks. "No." Nate catches my wrists, drawing my hands away from his groin. "I pay for sex." His fingertips press into my skin, his palms surprisingly rough. "I have to."

He has to. I tilt my head back and read the determination on his face. This isn't negotiable for Nate. If I want to touch the man of my dreams, I have to be paid for it.

I can't figure out why this is a bad thing.

"First clarification: I'm giving you a hand job. We're not having full-blown sex." I twist my arms, easily breaking his hold on my wrists. "Second clarification: of course you're paying for this." I roll my eyes. "You didn't think you were getting a freebie, did you?"

"You don't need money." Nate steps backward.

I follow him, not allowing his retreat. "I don't pay my landlord in peace signs and rainbows, sweetheart." I plunge my hand into the pocket of his pants. My fingertips touch soft cotton and my heart skips a beat.

My fastidiously neat man hasn't discarded the handkerchief I used this morning. He has kept the soiled fabric, carrying it around with him as he moves from meeting to meeting.

My chest warms. Nate cares for me. I'm not just any woman for him. This encounter is more than a businesslike exchange of money for sex.

I remove his wallet, giving no indication I've discovered his secret, and fan through the contents, acting cool and detached, professional.

"Dollar bills; how quaint," I quip, selecting a single twenty-dollar bill, thinking this should be payment enough. The hookers on TV charge by the hour and Nate won't last long, his body already primed for my touch.

I slowly slide his wallet into his pocket, pressing my fingers against him, teasing him, tormenting him. Nate shudders, his reaction immediate and gratifying.

"Don't come yet." I grin as I withdraw my hand. "I want you to get your money's worth." I unbutton my blazer and tuck the twenty-dollar bill into my corset. "There are no refunds."

Nate frowns, his gaze lingering on my breasts. "The others charge—"

I cover his grim lips with my right index finger. "I don't want to hear another word about the other women and what they charge or what they do." His eyes flash, bolts of lightning surging through his darkened irises. "They run their businesses their way. I run my business my way." I sweep my fingertip over his lips back and forth, back and forth. His breath blows tantalizingly hot against my skin. "This is a deposit. I'll collect the remaining balance after the transaction is completed."

I drift my hands over his suit-clad chest, relishing his firm muscle and solid form. "There will be none of that pay-in-sixty-days nonsense either." I swirl my fingers over his slim sleek belt buckle. "I expect immediate cash." I release his belt and he inhales sharply, his body shaking.

"I want cold hard cash." I stroke Nate through his pants, the rigid proof of his desire giving me confidence. He leans against the wall, pushing his hips forward, silently granting me permission to touch him.

I unzip him, the rasping sound loud in the quiet room, a declaration of erotic intention. He's mine for now, this stern serious man. I push his black pants and pristine white boxer shorts down to his knees, revealing the bloom of his cock head and his slightly curved shaft.

"Ahhh . . . so this is the true you, Nate." I trace his cock and he bobs. "You're not as straight as you want everyone to believe." I close my fingers around him, his veins pulsing under my fingertips. "You have some kink in you, don't you?"

His gaze lifts to my green hair. "Yes," he admits, his deep voice making my stomach flutter.

"I thought so." I pump him slowly, firmly, relishing the control I have over him, over his satisfaction. "Does it arouse you, knowing that outside this room employees are sitting at their desks, making business calls, sending e-mails?" I lean into him, lowering my voice. "They have no idea their CFO is being sexually serviced by a cock-loving intern, that my small pale fingers are wrapped around your big hard shaft, that I'm fucking you with my hands, wishing you were inside me."

Nate groans softly. "I won't last long." A bead of precum forms on his tip.

"I don't expect you to last long this first time." I brush my thumbs over him, spreading his essence, his skin glistening, his scent musky and male. "In the future you'll come only when I tell you to, understand?" He doesn't answer, his big chest rising and falling. "Understand?" I squeeze his base, my punishment pulling a sexy rumble from his lips, unlocking his last mental door.

"I understand." His eyes blaze with unguarded desire, his emotions opened to me, his soul exposed.

"Good." I run my hands up and down him, rewarding him for his concession. "You may be paying me, but I'm in control of our fuckfests. You don't know what you need. I do." Nate rocks into my hands. He needs to be pushed and I'm the woman to do it, to free him from his self-imposed incarceration. "I'm a professional." I smile at him, enjoying this new game, my authority over his body making me hot.

Nate grunts, the veins on his neck lifting, his golden skin covered with the sheen of perspiration. His hands are clenched into tight fists, his arms remaining by his sides.

"You can touch me if you wish." I arch my back, drawing his attention to my breasts. They ache for his fingers, my nipples painfully tight.

"Can't." Nate grimaces, moving faster against me, the muscles in his upper thighs flexing.

He can't touch me without losing control. This is how much he wants me.

"That's too bad." I roll his balls with my fingers, feeling strong, powerful, womanly. "My pussy is slick and wet, yearning to be filled with a big hard cock." I rub my thighs together, skin sliding over skin. "Can't you smell my need?"

"Yes." Nate inhales deeply, his nostrils flaring. "God, yes." He thrusts his hips again and again, humping my hand with an exciting savagery, his eyes feral and his motions erratic.

I match his intensity, tightening my grip on his cock, and this makes him wilder, his rhythm becoming grueling and harsh. Everyone else sees the cool, passionless Iceman. This is the true Nathan Lawford, this hot ardent man struggling to reach sexual satisfaction.

"Can't last," he huffs. "Need."

"Then take what you need." I grab a couple of tissues and cover his tip. "Come for me, Nate." I close the fingers of my left hand around his balls, ruthlessly pushing him toward completion.

Nate throws his head back and roars, driving his hips forward. I gaze at him with wonder, the force of his release awe-inspiring. Hot jets of cum pulse into the tissues, every surge draining more and more tension from his body.

Nate thrusts once, twice, shudders and stumbles backward, his shoulders smacking against the wall. He splays his fingers over the gray-painted surface, holding on, his eyes closed and his jaw relaxed.

I clean him carefully, lovingly. My neat executive doesn't like a mess. I toss the tissues into the wastebasket and pull up his boxer shorts and his pants, dressing him, restoring his armor of perfection, closing some of his doors.

"There." I pat his heaving chest. "You must feel better now, with all of that stress released." My frustration remains, my body throbbing with need.

Red streaks across Nate's cheeks. "I lost control." His voice is quiet.

"Good." I lean into him, pressing my hips against his. He doesn't touch me, doesn't wrap his arms around me. "That means I'm doing my job."

Nate opens his eyes, his expression glacier. "I never lose control."

He never loses control yet he lost control with me. I don't dare show my jubilation. My inflexible executive is perilously close to walking away from me, the source of his forbidden feelings.

"If you never lost control with the other women, then you never found true sexual release with them." I flatten my fingers over his jacket lapels, touching him, savoring him, not knowing if I'll get another chance, if he'll ever allow me to handle his big body again. "That must have been frustrating for you."

Lines etch between Nate's eyebrows.

"You won't have to worry about that with me," I assure him, giving him a cocky grin, high on my success. "With me you'll always lose control." I slip my hand into the pocket of his pants. "I know what you need, what you want, and I'll give it to you. Every time." I caress him through the fabric, sweeping my fingers along his hip as I remove his wallet.

"But my services aren't free." I study the wad of bills. How much money does an escort charge for a hand job? I chew on my bottom lip, having no idea. Twenty dollars hadn't been enough. I glance at Nate, hoping to read the answer in his eyes.

He sighs and takes the wallet from me, extracts an obscene amount of money. "This should settle my outstanding account." He holds out the bills.

I take the money, my heart pounding, and count it, curious about the amount. His outstanding account is more than I make in an entire day working at Blaine Technologies. I swallow my surprise and feign a frown. "You overpaid by twenty dollars." I return one of the bills to him.

Nate's lips twitch as he closes his fingers around the money. "I can't overpay. Pricing is determined by supply and demand. How did you pass your college economics class?"

How does he know I took an economics class at college? I tuck the remaining bills into my corset. "I gave the prof the answers I thought a normal person would." I glance at my phone. It's five minutes to one o'clock. "You have a meeting now so I'll forgive you this first time. But during future appointments I also expect to come."

Nate tilts his chin upward. "I've had no complaints."

"Until now." I plant my hands on my hips and glare up at him, the thought of him pleasuring other women irritating me. "Did you even kiss me, Nate? Touch me? Hookers have needs too."

He frowns. "All of the other women asked that I not kiss them."

Don't kiss the clients. Maintain some professional distance. I recall hearing that in a movie. "I run my business my way." I struggle to maintain my outraged expression. "And I like to be kissed. I—"

Nate hooks his arms around my waist, pulls me to him and captures my lips. I gasp, the force of his kiss driving my head back, and he surges inside me, sliding his tongue along mine. I cling to his shoulders as he explores, branding, owning my mouth, devouring me with an unmatched hunger, as though he hasn't tasted a woman in years.

Because he hasn't tasted a woman in years, perhaps in decades. I soften against him, shocked by this revelation. Escorts prefer not to be kissed and Nate has never been linked to anyone else. I suck on his tongue and he groans, rubbing his hands over my back, pressing my breasts against his chest.

I yield completely to Nate, giving him everything I have, the connection between us strengthening. This is why escorts don't kiss their clients. This intimacy is dangerous, something to be feared. I know no such caution, my reckless heart pushing me forward. I thread my fingers through Nate's short soft hair, and he cups my ass, lifting me into him, fusing our bodies together.

His breath wafts against my cheeks. His distinctive scent, his tantalizing body heat surrounds me. My lips hum and my jaw aches. I've never been kissed like this before, to the exquisite point of pain.

"You didn't lie in the elevator." Nate licks my throbbing bottom lip. "You do taste delicious." He mouths over my chin. "Spicy, hot, and exotic." He pulls on my skin.

His chest vibrates, his phone reminding him of his upcoming meeting.

"You have to go." I say what he won't. "We'll set up another appointment." I push him for a second encounter, knowing he'll rebuff my offer, telling me one time with freak-of-the-week Camille is enough.

"I'll set up the appointment." Nate lowers me until my feet touch the carpet. He'll set up the appointment. I stare

at him, stunned. He wants to see me again. "We'll negotiate the contract then," he adds.

"The contract?" My spine straightens. "Hell to the no."
I shake my head vigorously. "I don't do contacts." Contracts are a means of control. No one controls me.

"The contract can be ended at any time," Nate assures
me. "We'll lay down some rules. There will be no more
unmet expectations." He sweeps one of his thumbs over
my kiss-swollen lips, attempting to soothe me with his
seductive touch.

I can't be soothed. I'm strong, independent, free. "I
don't do rules either." I step backward, away from him,
away from temptation.

"The contract benefits you." The dogged determination reflected in Nate's eyes worries me. "It'll protect you."

"I don't need to be protected." Especially not from
him. Nate is one of the most honorable men I know. "And
I certainly don't need a contract."

"Miss Trent . . ."

"No contracts, Nate." I open the door and step into
the hallway. The air is cooler, clearing my passion-fogged
brain, forcing me to face my new reality. Blaine Technologies' sexy young CFO paid me for sex. I'm officially his
prostitute, his lady of the evening, his money honey.

I still can't figure out why this is a bad thing.

All I know is that Nate wants to see me again. I
walk away, my head held high and my hips swaying. He
wants me.

The tall, dark-haired lawyer Miss Yen hired to help
with the Volkov merger strides toward me. He normally

ignores me, the lowly intern. Today he treats me to one of his slimy thousand-dollar smiles, his gaze fixed on my bountiful bosom.

Am I giving off hooker vibes? I tug on my blazer. Can he smell the combination of sex and money?

"Green," Miss Yen hollers.

If tall, dark, and creepy has discerned what I've done, my boss will definitely know. Miss Yen has the freaky ability of being able to sense whenever I've broken a rule.

"Coming." I graze the door with my knuckles as I enter her office, mentally preparing myself for the confrontation.

She paces behind her desk. I perch on the edge of an extremely uncomfortable guest chair and wait as she burns a trail in the carpet, striding back and forth, back and forth. Miss Yen makes a hippie high on acid appear lethargic, my pint-sized boss bouncing around the office like a ping-pong ball.

Finally she sits down. "I don't want to lose another intern, but I have to do the right thing for Blaine Technologies. I know about your extracurricular activities, Green."

Flaming balls of feces. My mouth dries. She's confronting me about Nate.

"I can explain," I lie. I have no idea how I'll explain this.

"Let me explain first." Miss Yen stops my sure-to-be inadequate blabbering. "There *might* be a last-minute opening in this year's Change the World program." She slides a piece of paper toward me. "Fill out this application and you *might* have an opportunity to pitch your project at the end of the month."

I stare at the form, stunned. "There's an opening for the Change the World grant?" This isn't about Nate and me?

"There *might* be an opening," Miss Yen emphasizes. "There are no guarantees. This is, as you would say, a big maybe."

I'm not being fired and my project could be sponsored this year. The tension eases from my shoulders. "Does the program have to be operational?"

My boss' lips twist. "We don't fund dreams, Green."

I'm more interested in the mentoring than the funding. I don't have the skill set to make this project a success. I also won't make this deadline working alone. "I'll have to subcontract some of the work." The wad of cash nestled between my breasts will pay for this delegation of duties.

"I've drafted a standard subcontractor agreement template for Blaine Technologies." Miss Yen swivels in her chair, opens a drawer in one of the filing cabinets behind her, extracts more papers. "Take out the clauses that don't apply to you and tweak some of the information. If a concern isn't covered talk to me and I'll help you with the wording." She meets my gaze. "I know you like to bend the rules."

I open my mouth.

She raises her hand, stopping my token protest. "But resist that temptation. If even a hint of scandal is attached to your project, it won't be awarded funding."

Selling my body to pay for subcontractors definitely qualifies as a hint of scandal. "Yes, Miss Yen." I gather the papers and stand. "Thank you for this opportunity."

"This is a *potential* opportunity. It might not happen." Miss Yen glances away from me as though she is embarrassed by my gratitude. "And get those expense reports corrected first," she says gruffly.

I step toward the door.

"And Green?"

"Yes, Miss Yen?" I pause.

"Button up your blazer. I don't want to see your cleavage again." My boss turns her attention to her computer screen, dismissing me.

I glance downward. My breasts are one jiggle away from popping out of my corset. I hastily fasten the buttons, the mystery of my sudden popularity solved. A flash of bosom will snag the interest of even the most disapproving male. Nate is proof of that.

I return to my desk, set the application forms aside, and concentrate on the dreaded expense reports. Hours pass as I confirm line item after line item. Every expense, no matter how small, has been claimed by the penny-pinching lawyers. Every project has its own accounting code.

I wonder what Nate is doing and why I'm so obsessed with an unbending executive interested only in a sexual relationship. It'll be a great sexual relationship if his kisses are an indication of his skills. I touch my puffy lips, tasting him on my tongue. And he has a huge cock. I press my thighs together, imagining him inside me, filling me.

I resist the urge to touch myself. Instead, I take another photo of my breasts, flashing some perky pink nipple, and send the image to Nate. It will be a late night for me. I have the application forms to fill out, the subcontractors to hire, a price list of sexual acts to source. I want Nate to have an equally sleepless night thinking about me.

Chapter Three

THE NEXT MORNING I stand by Blaine Technologies' revolving doors, waiting as Jerome, my nemesis, searches my backpack. He's been harassing me for sixteen minutes while he allows more conservative-looking employees to heft car-sized briefcases into the office building.

I don't care.

Because Nate hasn't set up another appointment. He hasn't contacted me. At all. I sigh. He must have filled his quota of quirky and will be returning to his vanilla-sex women. He'll pay them to touch him, stroke him, please him.

Last night in an attempt to forget about Nate, to forget about the pain in my soul, I focused wholeheartedly on the data donation project, working until three in the morning.

This morning I don't have that distraction and I'm tired, too tired to think rationally, to process the emotions churning inside me.

"Will you be finishing this search sometime today?" I ask the security guard. The metal table in front of me is littered with the contents of my backpack. One of my screens has been scratched beyond repair.

"You should treat me with respect, Miss Trent." Jerome's slimy gaze sweeps my body, lingering on my breasts.

"Or what?" I mumble. "You'll make my life more miserable than it already is? That's not possible."

"Isn't it?" The security guard peels the top off my plastic lunch container. "What's this?" He sniffs. "It smells like drugs."

Great. Just when I thought this day couldn't get any worse, the rent-a-cop finds a new way to torture me.

Jerome licks his index finger and holds it up, his skin gleaming with his saliva. He then sticks his grubby finger into my yellow chicken curry and swirls it around, thoroughly contaminating my lunch.

"Nope, it's not drugs." He closes the container and hands my lunch to me. "You're free to go, Miss Trent." Jerome smirks. He folds his arms in front of his big belly and watches as I reassemble my bag, making no attempt to help me.

I sling the straps of my backpack over one of my shoulders and trudge toward the elevators, my mood as dark as my suit. My depression is silly. Our relationship, arrangement, whatever Nate and I have, was destined to end. I knew this.

The doors open. My indifferent executive stands in his usual corner, wearing his usual black suit, white shirt, black tie. He gazes at me blankly, his pale gray eyes revealing nothing, his emotions closed to me.

"Miss Trent." He offers me his normal greeting, the greeting he's given me for months, acting as though yesterday hadn't happened, as though nothing has changed.

I want him more than life and he doesn't care. At all.

"Nate." I stomp into the elevator and slap my palm against the button for the fifth floor. The doors close and the car jerks into motion.

He says nothing, his expression cold and withdrawn, untouchable.

"Bastard." I turn my back toward him and watch the red digital numbers change.

"Pardon?"

"You heard me." I tap my shoes against the tile, refusing to look at him. "I greet my enemies with more warmth than you greeted me. You came in my hand, lover boy. I held your cock, heard your groans, smelled your musk."

"What do you expect from me?" Nate asks quietly. I glance over my shoulder, see the confusion in his eyes.

I shake my head, not buying his act. "I expect you to make an appointment if you say you'll make an appointment. If you don't want me anymore I expect you to be a man and tell me."

"I want you."

Nate wants me. I should tell him to take a long walk off a short pier. I can't. Damn him. I burn for his touch, hunger for his lips, want him with every inch of my being. "Then make another freakin' appointment."

"I want you now." He strides forward, waves his pass-card over the control-panel sensor, and taps the emergency stop button. The elevator stops. "I can't wait to have you."

He has some nerve. I pivot on my heel. "Go to—"

Nate covers my moving lips with his, smothering my curse. My backpack drops to the tiled floor, the thud loud in the silence, and I slam my mouth shut, refusing him access for one heartbeat, clinging to my pride.

My token resistance doesn't dissuade Nate. He jabs his tongue into the seam of my lips, demanding entrance, bombarding me with a steady persistent assault.

No match for his determination, my emotional walls crumble and I open to him, allowing him inside me. Nate ravishes my mouth with his tongue, thrusting into me again and again, punishing me for my denial. He tastes of the mints he constantly chews, breathtakingly fresh, and I suck on his flesh, grasping his broad shoulders greedily with my hands. His muscles flex under my fingertips, his strength thrilling me.

Nate backs me against a wall, trapping me between hard mirror and harder man, and I swivel my hips, grinding against the ridge in his pants, molding my curves to his muscle. This isn't enough, not nearly enough, the layers of fabric between us frustrating me.

Nate grasps my left thigh and lifts my leg, hiking my skirt upward. I submit to his dominance, bending my knee, wrapping myself around him. My panties are soaked with my juices, my need for him spiraling upward, an uncontrollable volcano of passion. I rub my scent over his black pants, seeking to claim him as he is claiming me.

"Hot." Nate drags his mouth along my neck, blazing a trail of sensation across my skin. "You're so hot, so passionate." He reaches under my skirt, twists his fingers in my G-string panties, and tugs, tearing the delicate lace. "I need to feel you, feel your heat."

"Yes." I reach between us and unzip his pants, freeing him. Skin touches skin. A voice inside me warns that I'm forgetting something, something important, and I hesitate, not knowing what this something could be. This feels right. Nate feels right.

Nate shows no such uncertainty, no hesitation. He pushes against me, flattening me against the wall, and growls into my mouth, the animalistic sound exciting, raw, and real. He has lost control and is no longer my cool calm executive, a man governed by rules and rational thought. He's a primitive animal intent on mating, on capturing his female.

This can't be wrong. It's natural, meant to be, destined. I rub my pussy lips against Nate's shaft, wetting his skin, needing to be closer to him, to have him inside me. He cups my ass and raises my body higher, holding me over his hard cock. His tip bumps against my clit, setting off a ripple of bliss, and the contact silences my cautionary voice, leaving only a soul-deep need.

I'm desperate for him, for this. "Please." I clutch his arms, digging my fingertips into the rich fabric of his suit. "Take me."

Nate meets my gaze, his eyes dark and stormy, as turbulent as my desire. "You're mine, Camille." He drives me down on him, impaling me onto inches of unyielding shaft.

I shriek my dismay and struggle to be free. He's too large, too much, my pussy lips stretched around his girth, pain edging my pleasure.

"Made for me," Nate grunts, holding me tight, not allowing me to escape. I'm helpless to stop him as he continues his relentless surge upward, into me, his cock head brazing along my pussy walls, his size reshaping my body.

He captures my lips with his, filling my mouth with his tongue as he fills my pussy with his cock, owning me completely. I taste the freshness of his mouth. I feel the bloom of his broad tip, the curve of his shaft, the raised veins on his skin. I inhale his clean scent.

His base presses against me and the invasion temporarily stops. Before I can catch my breath and adjust to his size, he pulls out and slams back inside me. My bare ass slaps against the mirrored wall, the sting causing my pussy to clench around him.

Nate groans into my mouth and repeats the motion, taking me harder. I gasp and cling to him, wrapping my legs around his waist, linking my ankles over his ass. He rides me against the wall, his urgency feeding mine. Skin smacks against skin. My hips, pussy, and ass burn, heating at the points of contact. My legs tremble.

Nate wrenches his lips away from mine, his chest rising and falling against my breasts. "You feel so good." He drops his head to my left shoulder, driving into me with a breathtaking force. "So fucking good."

I've never heard Nate drop the f-bomb. This is how far gone he is, how far gone we both are. We're rutting in the company elevator, uncaring about the security cameras, about our coworkers, about the silly game we've been playing.

I look over his shoulder and gaze with awe at our reflections in the mirror. My black heels bounce against Nate's clenched ass cheeks, his skin golden and perfect, the muscles in his legs flexed and defined. His head is lowered, his face presses against my neck, his blond hair contrasting vividly against my green strands. My face is flushed, my eyes glassy, my kiss-swollen lips parted.

I've never seen myself like this before, have never felt this way about a lover, crazed and out of control. And Nate *is* my lover. It doesn't matter how much he pays me. It won't change my feelings. I turn my head and suck on his skin, tasting salt and man, my man.

He shudders and fucks me faster, taking me harder, our bodies colliding, smashing together. Each thrust of his hips shreds more of my control. Tremors sweep my body, pushing me closer to fulfillment.

"Come for me, Camille." Nate drives deep, filling me completely. "Come." He makes a circular motion with his hips, grinding against my clit.

I scream, shattering into a thousand jagged pieces, sharp shards of pleasure piercing my form. Nate bellows my name and pins me against the wall, shooting hot cum into my battered pussy, his release setting off another wave of bliss. I buck, writhe, twist. He leans his physique into mine, pressing me flat, restraining me with his muscle.

I cease moving, too drained, too satisfied to fight him. The elevator stops spinning around me. My heartbeat slows. Nate holds me against the wall, his cock remaining inside me, the connection between us humming.

"I like this arrangement." I smile, feeling warm and sleepy and sexually sated, my rough edges smoothed.

Nate raises his head and his eyes widen. "Condoms."

"What?" I blink.

"We forgot to use condoms." He lowers my feet to the floor and staggers backward. "I never forget to use condoms."

Shit. I knew this encounter would come back to bite me in the ass. "I'm clean." I smooth my skirt down, his essence coating my thighs, his warmth filling me. "And I'm on birth control."

"Birth-control pills aren't one hundred percent effective." He yanks his pants upward and fastens them, his movements sharp and angry. "That's why I only deal with professionals." Nate glares at his reflection in the mirrored wall. "They always use condoms."

They always use condoms. They never kiss. I chew on my bottom lip. "Your sex life must have sucked big time."

"This isn't funny." Nate rakes his fingers through his hair. He's extremely upset.

"No, this isn't funny," I concede. "But this also isn't your problem. It's mine. I'll take care of any possible consequences."

"You'll take care of any possible consequences?" He snorts. "I've driven by the apartment building you call home. You can't even take care of yourself."

I stare at him. My apartment building is situated in a very bad area of town. No one casually drives by it unless he's armed with semiautomatic weapons.

"I'll handle this." Nate releases the emergency stop button and the elevator recommences its ascent, the red digital numbers changing.

I frown. "There might not be anything for you to *handle*." His jaw juts and I grow alarmed. "Nothing has to be decided now," I emphasize.

"I want exclusivity."

"What?" My lips part.

"Until this matter is resolved, no other man will touch you," Nate states, a possessive gleam in his eyes. "I'll pay for all of your time." He pauses. "I want to ensure the child is mine."

It's not like him to explain his decisions, and there are other ways to verify a child is his. Nate is an intelligent man. He knows this. I tilt my head. He's asking for exclusivity because he *wants* to be the only man touching me.

He wants a month-long commitment. At the end of this month I'll either be over my Iceman obsession or have my heart shattered. A normal woman would run away from this no-win scenario.

There's nothing normal about me. "Exclusivity works both ways," I tell him. "You're not to touch any other women."

"I agree." Nate nods, giving his acquiescence surprisingly quickly. He reaches into his suit jacket, retrieves his phone, taps on the screen. "We're both free at noon. I'll schedule a meeting to finalize the contract. We'll want it signed today."

His eagerness to lock me in scares and excites me. "I don't do contracts."

"You should always do contracts. It's risky to supply services without one." Nate reaches into his pocket again. "I could walk away now and not pay you."

He hands me a green money clip stretched wide with cash, reminding me who I am to him. I'm his prostitute, a woman he thinks he's bought.

I still don't know why this is a bad thing.

"I could hack into your bank account and pay myself." I grip the cash. He prepared the payment in advance. He planned for our encounter. I thumb through the folded bills, pretending to count the money, uninterested in the total. "You overpaid by twenty dollars."

"I always overpay by twenty dollars." Nate's lips curl into his version of a smile. "You can earn that money at noon."

I don't know if I can wait that long, my desire for Nate already consuming me. "I'll earn that money in a minute, darling." The elevator doors open at my floor. "Twenty dollars doesn't buy you squat."

I hear a chuckle as I walk away. It couldn't have come from Nate's lips. The Iceman never laughs.

My spirits are high and I'm extra loud with my morning greetings, earning me four shushings, two tongue clucks, and one "For goodness' sake. Some people are trying to work."

"Green," Miss Yen yells. No one dares to shush her.

I march into her office and plunk my ass down on one of the guest chairs. Sitting in a small confined space with my overly observant boss is high risk. I'm not wearing panties, I smell like sex, and I have a money clip the size of a transport truck stuffed in my cleavage.

Miss Yen stands behind her desk, her phone pressed to her ear. She's wearing yet another formfitting black suit. It's beautiful and likely expensive, the same type of suit Nate's women-for-hire often wear.

I tug on my ill-fitting blazer and my fingernails break through the thinning fabric. My shoulders droop. I don't have time to shop for a replacement suit.

"I have to reschedule. Something came up." Miss Yen scowls at me as she talks on the phone. I'm definitely in deep doo-doo.

"Yes, two o'clock will work. Thank you." She slams the phone down on the desk. "Mr. Henley requested an eight o'clock meeting." Miss Yen crosses her arms. "Do you have any idea why Blaine Technologies' head of cybersecurity would want to see me?"

I have many ideas as to why Mr. Henley might want to see my boss. They range from yet another complaint from Jerome, his oppressive security guard, to the stinky food issue. "I could find out for you," I offer, sidestepping the question.

"No, don't *find out* for me," Miss Yen snaps. "Don't open files you shouldn't have access to. Don't snoop in other people's e-mail boxes. Don't *borrow* passcards or break into stairwells." She lists some of my past crimes. "Sit at your desk and finish the expense reports."

"Yes, Miss Yen." I slink out of her office, clunk my backpack into one of my desk drawers, and slump into my seat. A cloud of floral perfume hangs over my cubicle, the stench originating from the pinch-faced lady's desk.

I peruse an expense report, Miss Yen's anger sucking all of the joy out of my encounter with Nate. When I first joined Blaine Technologies I thought working here would be different. Gabriel Blaine, the founder and CEO, is a former hacker, a man who thumbed his nose at the establishment and paid the price, spending some time in the slammer for freeing information.

I match expenses to receipts. Mr. Blaine's chief of security, Mr. Henley, is one of the top experts in the world and is a man known to do anything, and I mean *anything*, to keep his people safe. I respect his sense of purpose.

Nate is more badass than Mr. Blaine and Mr. Henley combined. My favorite CFO might follow rules, but they are his rules. He wants to pay for sex? He pays for sex, potential jail time be damned. He wants to fuck a green-haired rebel chick in the company elevator? He fucks a green-haired rebel chick in the company elevator. Screw the security cameras.

I open the electronic report and adjust one of the values in the expense form. All of the totals change, requiring me to reprint and reconfirm the numbers. I march over to the printer, grab the paper, and return to my seat.

The executives aren't a bad bunch and I could even put up with nasty people like Jerome and the pinch-faced lady. It's the excessive rules that drive me batty. We have to wear dark suits. We must start work at eight o'clock. We can't access certain areas, including the stairwells, the entire fourth floor, and Nate's locked office.

I spot Mr. Henley as the big man lumbers down the hallway, his head, neck, and shoulders visible over the cubicle walls. He has an ominous frown on his scarred face.

I hunch over the expense reports, hiding from him. If he can't find me he can't fire me. That's my theory.

The door to Miss Yen's office closes. Closed-door meetings never impart good news. I check off expense totals as I confirm them.

My phone buzzes. I glance at the small screen. Nate has sent me an invitation for the noon meeting, the subject being customer satisfaction. I mark the meeting as tentative, not knowing if I'll have a job in four hours. Less than a minute later the meeting status is changed to mandatory.

I laugh. Nate is a bossy, bossy man, and he's thinking about me.

The pinch-faced lady hisses at me, my work neighbor irritated by my happiness. I dig my lunch out of my backpack—the curry Jerome, the security guard, contaminated—and open the lid, allowing the fragrant spices to escape.

My nemesis hisses even louder, sounding as though she has an air leak. I replace the lid, my mission accomplished, and focus on the expense reports. I have one more set to verify and I want to complete this task before I get fired.

Miss Yen's office door opens. I work faster, totaling the last column in record time.

"Green," my boss yells mere seconds after I set the last expense report on the top of the pile. The pinch-faced lady cackles. She knows I'm in big trouble.

I dump my entire lunch into the wastebasket, put the empty container in my backpack, and trudge to my boss' office. "You wanted to see me, Miss Yen?"

"No, I don't want to see you, but I have to see you, don't I?" Miss Yen bows her body over her desk, rubbing her temples, appearing defeated. "Sit." First I break Nate. Now I've broken the dragon lady. I don't know whether to be proud or dismayed.

I fill the nearest guest chair and lean back, stretching my legs. Past experience has taught me that being fired takes a long time. I might as well get comfortable.

"What is your relationship with Mr. Lawford?" Miss Yen lifts her head and meets my gaze.

My body temperature drops. She's found out about Nate and me. "Mr. Lawford is Blaine Technologies' CFO," I quip, buying time as I figure out a game plan. My job is a goner, but I might be able to save Nate's position.

"Drop the innocent act, Green." Miss Yen leans toward me. "There are security cameras in the shredding room."

"Oh." I chew on my bottom lip, thinking quickly. "It's all my fault." I take the blame.

"I know who is responsible." Miss Yen shakes her head. "In the eight years I've known Mr. Lawford, he has never acted inappropriately."

I stare at Miss Yen. She doesn't know about the escorts. She believes his squeaky-clean Iceman image.

"There was also a transfer of money caught on video." Miss Yen lowers her gaze to my chest, and I shift nervously in my chair, aware that I have Nate's money clip tucked into my corset. "Some people might see that footage and think Mr. Lawford was being blackmailed."

I swallow hard. "I wouldn't hurt Nate. I believe in peace and love." I form a V with my fingers and smile brightly, trying to diffuse the situation.

"You also believe in chaos and anarchy." Miss Yen studies me closely. I drop my hand. I'm not fooling anyone, especially not my keen-eyed boss.

"And you have a unique way of solving problems," she continues. "Mrs. Blaine and Miss Volkov, your friends, are both in happy relationships. It's understandable that you want that same happiness for yourself." My boss nods as though she has me all figured out. She has no freakin' clue. Even I haven't figured myself out.

"But this isn't the way to do it, Green." Miss Yen tilts her body forward, her expression uncharacteristically gentle. "A relationship built upon threats won't last."

I blink. "You think I'm blackmailing Nate into a relationship?"

She hesitates for a heartbeat and then nods. "Money and sex are two powerful ways to control a man."

"Or to control a woman." A trickle of sweat drips down my spine. "That clever bastard. He wants to change me, doesn't he? Make me into someone I'm not, someone he thinks he can love." Tension stretches across my shoulders. I can't be that person. My true nature always shines through. "That's what you're saying, right?" I look at Miss Yen.

She gazes at me as though I've lost my mind.

Because I *have* lost my mind. "What am I talking about?" I laugh loudly. "He's Nathan Lawford. He's wealthy, intelligent, good-looking. He can have any woman he wants." My shoulders lower as my anxiety dissipates. "Why would he go to the hassle of changing a green-haired rebel child?"

"I thought you were responsible for the activities in the shredding room." Miss Yen lifts her eyebrows.

"I am. It was all me." I wave my hands. "I never follow the rules."

"You should follow the rules in the future." Miss Yen sighs. "Get back to work and try to stay out of trouble."

I scurry out of Miss Yen's office before she changes her mind. For some unknown reason she isn't firing me. I won't question this good luck.

The hallway smells like curry, and the pinch-faced lady mutters dire threats as she sprays rose-scented deodorizer into the air. I return to my desk, knot the top of the garbage bag, and carry the remains of my lunch to the break room. I still have a job. My work neighbor will have to deal with my ethnic food, at least for one more day.

Chapter Four

I WAIT UNTIL ten minutes to twelve, gather the expense reports, and walk to the elevators. The pinch-faced lady has already warmed up her broccoli, the hallway reeking of booty bombs. Thanks to Jerome, the nasty security guard, I have no lunch.

I hope Nate has ordered something for our meeting. It won't be a tasty something. I've arranged meals for Miss Yen's lunch meetings. These orders normally consist of fancy sandwiches and macaroni salad, the choices as appetizing as the china plates on which they're served. At this point I'm not fussy. Even thinly shaved roast beef stuffed into a white roll will take the edge off my hunger.

I push the elevator up button five times, and the doors open as though the elevator has been waiting for me. Three dark-suited corporate clones huddle against the mirrored wall, the same mirrored wall Nate fucked me against that morning.

We'll fuck again in this meeting. This is the sweetest gig I've ever landed. I'm being paid outrageous amounts of cash to boink the man of my dreams.

I still can't figure out why this is a bad thing.

The tallest clone clears his throat. "You're going to the seventh floor," he observes. Freckles are sprinkled across his rosy face. "That's the finance department." He pauses and I wait. He says nothing, gazing at me expectantly.

I remember I have a role to play. I'm his boss' money honey. "I know that's the floor for the finance department," I purr in my most seductive voice, fully embracing my inner sex goddess. "Accountants make me hot."

"T-t-they do?" he squeaks. The other two corporate clones stare at me.

"Oh yes." I trace the edges of the expense reports slowly, sensually. "There's nothing sexier than a man with a head." I drop my gaze to his groin. "For numbers." I lick my bottom lip.

"I—I—I . . ." he stammers, beads of sweat forming on his forehead.

I smother my smile. Breaking Nate's employee is surprisingly satisfying. "But a coworker of yours is a big meanie." I pout, curling my pierced bottom lip. "He rejected all of my expense reports and my boss yelled at me."

"No!" the clones collectively gasp.

"Yes." I examine each man, allowing my gaze to linger over their bodies, imagining they're Nate. "If he rejects the reports again I'm scared I'll get fired, and I won't ever see any of you again."

"T-t-that won't happen." The shortest clone steps forward. "Give me your expense reports, miss, and I'll take care of them for you."

"No, I will," the other two men volunteer in unison.

"Can you do that?" I flutter my eyelashes. "Are you that powerful?"

"Yes," all three of them assure me.

"That would be," I sigh, my breasts rising and falling, "positively heroic." The elevator doors open and I hold out the expense reports. The tallest clone grabs them first. "Thank you, boys." I wiggle my ass as I exit, the doors closing behind me.

"Hi." I smile at Gladys, the gatekeeper. The elderly woman who guards Nate's domain sits behind a painstakingly neat black lacquer desk. Her plump form is clad in a simple ebony suit. Glasses are perched on the tip of her button nose. "I have a twelve o'clock appointment with Nate."

"You may go in, Miss Trent. *Mr. Lawford* is expecting you," she subtly corrects me, her pink lips pursed with disapproval.

"Thank you, *Gladys*." I stride over the threshold and trek at a fast clip along the hallway, unencumbered by the expense reports. The finance floor resembles the legal floor, the walls, carpet, and cubicles gray, the layout similar. Multiple printers hum and voices whisper. I sniff the air, smelling curry, beef teriyaki, and oranges. Maybe we won't be eating plastic sandwiches after all.

An Asian woman leans into the hallway, stares at me, and then draws her head back into her cubicle. I hear her hushed tones as I pass her desk. A tall thin man stands, gazes at me, ducks down again. This happens again and again, a river of murmurs following me.

Nate's office door is open. I rap my knuckles on the wood and sweep into his private space. "Nate."

"Miss Trent." He sits in a black leather captain's chair, looking obscenely handsome, impeccably neat, and completely untouchable. I gaze at him with open admiration. His pale gray eyes are glacier, every strand of his golden hair is perfect, and he's mine. This gorgeous successful man is mine.

I tear my gaze away from him and look around his office. Nate's desk dominates one end of the space, his computer screens displaying colorful bar graphs. A wall of business books is shelved behind him. The guest chairs appear comfortable. I pivot on my heel. The floor-to-ceiling windows are uncovered, the sun streaming through the glass. The locked filing cabinets tempt me. The artwork is—

I stop, my heart squeezing.

At first glance the painting is merely an arrangement of monochromatic numbers, the shades ranging from the palest gray to the darkest black. I look longer, deeper, and see the hidden image. A woman cradles her baby in her arms, the expression on her face serene and loving. "Oh, Nate, they're beautiful."

The door clicks closed. "No one else sees them." He stands beside me. His face is carved out of ice, a mask hiding his true feelings, protecting him.

"They see with their minds, not with their hearts." Unlike me. Unlike Nate. I slip my fingers into his palm.

This is another one of his secrets, a bit of his soul exposed. "I won't tell anyone," I promise.

We gaze at the painting together, the room quiet except for the sound of our breathing. His clean, freshly showered scent fills my nostrils and his heat coils around my body. A tranquility, a sense of rightness falls over me. This is where I'm meant to be.

"I want a month." Nate breaks the silence. "And I want sole custody of our child if you're pregnant. You may visit whenever you wish, but our child lives with me."

He's serious. He's demanding custody of our imaginary child. I open my mouth.

Nate holds up his hand, stopping my words. "I know you might not be pregnant, but I won't take that chance, Miss Trent. I won't have any child of mine believe she's not wanted."

I stare at him. "I'd want our child." I'm definitely having my heart shattered in a month.

"A bedroom in our house will always be available for you." He leads me to a guest chair. I sit on one side of the desk and he sits on the other, the positioning declaring us adversaries. "Our child will have proof in writing that I want her." He pushes a stack of papers toward me. "She'll never doubt it."

Did Nate doubt he was wanted? His parents, like mine, have never married, but unlike mine, his parents no longer live together. Did they love each other, love him?

I gaze down at the thick stack of papers and my jaw drops. "*This* is the contract?" My full name, Camille

Joplin Trent, and my complete address are listed on the first of many, many pages. "It's huge."

I don't hide my dismay. Long contracts are normally drafted when one or more parties have to make significant concessions. I doubt Nate plans to alter his life for me.

"Take your time." Nate leans back in his chair. "And read it. If you have any questions, any concerns, we'll talk about them. I want you to be happy."

"I'd be happier with no contract." I fan the pages, the legalese making my eyes cross and my head hurt. "I trust you, Nate. Don't you trust me?"

"This is about setting expectations, not trust." His jaw juts.

He's not moving on this. He wants a contract. I take deep breaths. I can do this . . . for him. "What should I know?" I clasp his black fountain pen, focusing on the sleek barrel and finely crafted nib, trying to ignore the anxiety building inside of me.

"I mentioned the sole custody," Nate coolly states, oblivious to my impending meltdown. "I'll have exclusivity. This is the per diem rate." He flips the pages and I gape. The per diem is more than I make in a week working at Blaine Technologies.

"You've overpaid by twenty dollars." I force my jibe, my voice flat.

Nate's eyes gleam. "I factored for that." He points at the line. "You won't have any living expenses. You'll share my house."

"We'll be living together?" I meet his gaze, unable to

conceal my surprise. No man has ever asked me to live with him.

"You'll share my house," Nate repeats. I frown, not knowing what it means. Is there a difference between living together and sharing a house? "I'll pay for your food, supply your clothing, provide your transportation," he adds.

"In other words you'll control everything I do." I drop the pen onto the wooden desktop. "Hell no." I push the contract toward him, my palms moist. "My freedom isn't for sale." I stand, preparing to run far away from him, from this deal. "Not at any price."

"I don't want your freedom." Nate steps in front of the door, blocking my exit. "And I don't want to control you. You'll have keys to my house and can come and go as you please. You determine what you eat or wear. You can refuse my advances at any time."

"Right." I snort. "And if I refuse all of your advances?" I lift my chin, calling his bluff.

"Then it will be a very long month," Nate says quietly.

It will be a very long month for both of us. He knows I can't resist him. I pivot on my heels and walk to the windows, confused, trusting the man but not the contract. What does Nate want?

He can't want me, the true me. No one wants a rebel. "You can't change me." I stare at the white fluffy clouds floating freely across the blue sky.

I tried to change for the other girls in the commune, for my classmates in school, for my first three boyfriends, and for countless others, striving to be less defiant, less passionate, less me.

Those changes never stuck, never became permanent, never felt natural or right. It was too difficult to be someone I wasn't, and eventually the true me resurfaced, betraying, hurting, angering the people around me, the people who trusted me, who believed in my manufactured façade.

I can't do that to Nate. I can't see that look in his eyes.

"I don't want to change you," he murmurs into my right ear, his voice deep. He rubs my back, his touch warm and soothing.

"You say that yet you want me to sign a contract, to follow your rules." I stretch my arms along the window, splaying my fingers on the glass, resting my right cheek against the cool surface. This is as close to being outside, to being free, as I can manage.

"We're setting expectations. I'm protecting you." Nate moves his hands in gentle circles, unknotting my muscles, restoring my calm. "You don't have to change. I promise you."

He promises me. Nate always keeps his promises. The tightness around my chest eases. My breathing levels. He doesn't want to change me.

Maybe he's tired of his vanilla-sex yes-women. Maybe I'm a vacation for him, a unique sexual experience. Maybe, just maybe, he'll be the man who finally accepts me for me, who loves me.

I'd be a fool not to chance it. The alternative is a lifetime alone. "I need to have my own things."

"Give me your security codes and your keys and I'll have the entire contents of your apartment moved today,"

Nate vows. "I'll also transfer funds into your bank account daily." He pulls the elastic out of my hair and threads his fingers through the green strands. "You can verify your balance whenever you want."

I'll have my things reminding me who I am, what I stand for. I don't care about the money. "If you try to change me you'll be unsuccessful," I warn.

Nate chuckles. "If I tried to change you I'd be a fool." He reaches around me and unbuttons my blazer. "Our arrangement lasts a month, Camille." He slips the garment off my shoulders and more of my tension dissipates. "Give me thirty days."

Thirty days is all he wants because a normal man like Nate won't ever seek a permanent relationship with a screwed-up rebel child like me. He won't ever love me. I'm merely a short-term fling for him, Nate's version of a back-alley fuck.

He's more than that for me, much more. I gaze at the sky, wishing I could fly away from the pain that is sure to come. Nate unzips my skirt and the fabric falls to the floor. I'm nude from the waist down, cold air wafting over my bare ass cheeks.

"What are you doing?" I glance over my shoulder, distracted by his actions, his proximity, his everything. I want him again, always.

"I'm freeing you." Nate skims his fingers over my corset, his touch relayed through the thin leather, branding my skin, owning me. "Showing the world how special you are."

He cups my breasts, squeezing and releasing, squeezing and releasing, and my body pulses to his rhythm, my nipples puckering into rigid points, my pussy moistening.

"Everyone returning from lunch can see you standing here." He nuzzles into the curve where my neck meets my shoulders and I tremble, the contact divine. "They see me touch you."

"Do you want our coworkers to see us together?" I move my feet farther apart, opening my stance, giving our imaginary audience a better view of my cleanly shaven mons, my pink pussy lips, my pale legs. Nate's golden fingers spread possessively over my black corset, claiming my form as his.

"Do you want them to see you fondle the company rebel?" I lean into him, my curves framed by his muscle. Nate strokes downward, over my breasts, ribs, stomach, and I quiver, needing his fingers lower, inside me. "To watch us as we fuck?"

"Yes," he rumbles, gliding his hands over my mons, palming my bare skin. "I want them to know you're mine."

He says all of the right words, expressing my secret fantasy, that a man like him would want to claim a woman like me, be proud to call me his, not want to change me in any way.

"For the next month this pussy belongs to me." Nate strums me, making my nerve endings hum, teasing my clit with lingering light caresses. "No other man will touch your softness." He mouths along my neck, his lips hot and firm. "Taste your skin."

"Only you." I sway, brushing my ass over the hard ridge in his dress pants, seeking to torment him as he's tormenting me.

"Only me." Nate dips his fingertips into my wetness and I jerk. The contact is too intense, too deliciously sublime, his rough, callused skin stimulating all of my senses.

"Easy," he murmurs. His lips vibrate against my earlobe, setting off tremors inside of me. "I have you, Camille." He pushes deeper, forging onward, relentless in his domination of me.

"Nate." I wiggle, dancing in place, eager for this, for him.

"You're so responsive." He nips my right earlobe. A ripple of pleasure cascades down my body, and I clench around his finger. "Tight." Nate plunges into my snug hold, forcing me to open for him. "Made for me," he rumbles, his chest pressing against my spine. "For this." He pumps me, drawing more moisture from my core, more bliss from my body.

"Yes." I move with him, shamelessly rocking into his palm, selfishly seeking my own release. I'm wanton, wild, needy. "Fill me, Nate." The heel of his hand presses against my clit and I tremble, the contact direct and constant. "I'm so empty."

"I'll fill you." He adds another finger, stretching me wider, and I whimper with delight, the fullness magnificent. "I'll give you this." He skims along me, setting off mini tsunamis of desire, the waves pulling me deeper and deeper under the surface. "I'll give you everything."

I'm drowning, breathless with need. Seeking relief, I pull my corset lower, freeing my breasts, the cool air tightening my nipples even more.

Nate sucks in his breath. "Beautiful." His appreciation excites me. He works my pussy with a renewed vigor while I clutch my curves, the dual assault pushing me closer and closer to climax, to sweet release.

"Nate." I don't want to come alone.

"Tell me what you need, Camille." He fucks me hard with his fingers, my pussy humming from his sweet abuse, my wetness bathing my thighs. "And I'll give it to you."

I bend over, pushing my bare ass into his pants-covered hardness. "I want you inside me." I grip the strips of metal that hold the panes of glass in place, the bars as rigid as my lover. "Give me every delectable inch." I roll my hips, seeking to entice him. "I want all of you."

"You want my cock." Nate withdraws his fingers, leaving a frustrating void inside me. "My cum." His zipper rasps, the sound loud in the quiet room. Fabric rustles. "Everything." Warm flesh bumps against my wet pussy lips.

"Yes." I tilt my hips, opening myself to him. "Everything."

"Everything," Nate repeats, pushing inside me, his size daunting. I've taken him once. His fingers fold over my hips. I know I can take him again. I clench the window frame, gazing at the sky as he fills my pussy with his cock, scorching me with heat and hardness.

I part my lips, sucking in oxygen, my wild eyes reflected in the glass. Anyone standing on the sidewalk, looking upward, will see Nate claim my body, my pale skin meshing with his golden tan, my breasts bare and my nipples taut.

The slow slide stops and he stills, his cock pulsing inside of me, every pump of blood through his veins relayed, the fit incredibly snug. "Perfect." Nate supplies the right word. We might be opposites in all other ways, but when we fuck we become one. With Nate I fit.

This is the feeling I've been looking for my entire life, this sense of belonging. A normal woman would wish to prolong it. She'd embrace Nate's slow pace, his unhurried movements, the way he leisurely pulls out and eases back inside of her.

I'm not a normal woman and I push back as I always do, bumping against him, urging him to take me harder, faster, frustrated by his restraint. I want to come now, damn it, not some time tomorrow.

Nate, my obstinate man, refuses to fuck me faster, advancing and retreating, advancing and retreating, his rhythm steady, ruthlessly regulated. He's sticking to his plan, thinking he's in control.

Fine. I'll allow him this illusion for a few more minutes. I sway into Nate, following his lead, waiting and waiting and waiting until he relaxes, until he eases his grip on my hips.

Then I clench down on him, squeezing his shaft with my inner muscles, pushing him as I push everyone, forcing a response.

"Fuck." Nate thrusts deep, smacking his hips against

my ass. He rides me hard for several satisfying moments, and I pant with happiness, my hold on his cock loosening, a fine sheen of moisture covering my near-naked body.

Nate is Nate, though, stubborn to the core. He won't change his plans for me or for anyone else. He slows his pace once more, reestablishing his control over me, over his own body, his restored restraint presenting a challenge I can't resist.

I constrict around Nate again and he growls, driving into me deeper and deeper, slapping his balls against my skin, digging his fingers into my hips. His punishment invigorates instead of subdues me. I laugh and buck backward, throwing myself fully into the encounter, heart, body, and soul.

As we fuck, rutting like wild animals against the windowpane, condensation forms on the glass and my world narrows to Nate's cock in my pussy, his hands on my body, his grunts echoing in the quiet office. I cling to the metal frame, my knuckles whitening, my body shaking with the force of his thrusts.

Nate bends over me, the soft fabric of his suit, the silk of his tie, the cotton of his shirt sliding along my exposed skin. He's fully dressed from the waist up, very much the powerful executive. I'm wearing my corset and heels, shamelessly exposed, his escort, a woman he's hired to service him, to pleasure him.

I will pleasure him. I undulate under Nate, loving him with every inch of me, not holding anything back. He cups my breasts, his hands large and rough, his hold on me confident and secure, and I arch my back, pressing into his palms, needing more sensation, more of him.

"Come for me." Nate pinches my nipples. The sharp tinge of pain is delectable, propelling me precariously close to satisfaction.

"Make me come," I gasp, the rebel inside of me daring him, wishing for him to prove his worth, to push back.

My challenge doesn't daunt Nate, not even for a second. He ravishes my pussy with control-damaging thrusts, severing my hold on reality, his hard muscle colliding with my soft curves.

We breathe heavily as we fight for our shared release, my lungs straining for oxygen. I'm hanging over an emotional precipice, ready to fall, my pussy humming, my knuckles aching, my knees threatening to buckle under me. I grit my teeth, shaking with need. I won't come without him. I can't.

"Camille." Urgency edges Nate's voice. "Please." He sucks on my right shoulder, his lips firm and hot.

He's asking for permission to come, giving me complete control over his body. "Two more thrusts and then come for me," I instruct, my deviant soul unable to simply relent, accept, let be. "Come hard."

A disgruntled rumble rolls up Nate's chest. He pulls out of me, brazing his cock head along my inner walls, dragging his mouth over my back, and a tremor rocks my form.

"One." He drives into my pussy, filling me completely, and I whimper, holding onto the window with everything I have, my desire too acute, too exquisitely real.

Nate leisurely withdraws, deliberately tormenting me, his movements aggravatingly slow. I squeeze my eyes shut and a teardrop of frustration drips down one of my cheeks, leaving a salty trail on my skin. He covers my lips with his right palm, his secure grip stimulating me even more.

"Two," Nate roars, thrusting deep. As his base slams against my pussy lips, he bends down and bites my shoulder, marking my body.

The unexpected pain breaks me, splintering my mind into a million fragments. I scream into Nate's hand, his skin muffling my sounds of ecstasy, his warmth rushing into me. It's too much. I can't hold on, can't remain standing. I plunge headfirst toward the carpet, falling, falling, falling into the abyss.

Nate wraps one of his arms around me and pulls me back, holding me, a firm steadfast presence amid the chaos, a stabilizing force in a whirlwind of desire. With him I'm free to fly. He'd never allow me to crash, never allow me to be hurt.

I stand, staring at the blue sky, Nate's breath on my neck, his fingers splayed over my breasts, his warmth inside me. The euphoria fades, reality returns, yet the feeling of freedom, of belonging remains.

Nate licks the mark on my shoulder, his tongue rough and arousing. "I hurt you," he murmurs, concern in his voice, concern for me, the green-haired freak.

He will hurt me. Eventually. A cautious woman would end this relationship now, before her heart was completely broken.

Caution has never been a strength of mine. "You branded me with your teeth." I turn in Nate's arms and gaze up at his handsome face, unable to walk away from him, from the possibility of forever. "I belong to you now," I declare. "I guess I'll have to sign your contract." The decision feels right.

"I guess you'll have to." Nate's stormy eyes gleam with a primitive satisfaction. "You should read it first, though, know what you're signing."

"I trust you." Reading a contract requires thinking, and this is a decision to be made with my heart, not my brain. I stride to his desk, clad in my corset and heels. Nate pulls up his pants, fastens them, and follows me, fully dressed.

"Where do I sign?" I lean over the desk and Nate curves one of his palms possessively over my bare ass, his skin deliciously warm and rough.

He flips to the last page and points to the line. "You should read it first."

"I never do what I should." I scrawl my name on the delectably fine linen paper, filling the entire space with my flamboyant signature. The deed is done. My stomach flutters. There's no backing out of our arrangement now.

"Thank you."

Nate's sincerity reassures me. I've made the right decision. He needs this contract for some unknown reason.

"Don't thank me yet." I force my light tone. "Because I'm keeping your pen." I clip it to my corset, the gold cold against my heated skin. "It'll be a souvenir from the day I sold myself into sexual servitude."

My joke falls flat. Nate's joy fades, his face growing grim. "You should read the contract."

I tilt my head back and study him, not knowing what I said wrong. "*You* should uphold the contract and feed me." My stomach rumbles, emphasizing my point, and I laugh. "I'm starving. You might want to hurry our lunch order."

Chapter Five

"LUNCHTIME APPOINTMENTS ARE the best." I sit in one of Nate's guest chairs, clad in my corset and heels, my legs hooked over the armrests, my body open to his gaze. We spent the hour eating and talking. To be more accurate, I talked and Nate listened, my executive growing more and more cold and withdrawn.

"Tomorrow we could have a picnic." I nibble on a piece of naan, enjoying the flatbread, undaunted by his silence. Nate surprised me with spicy Indian food, dishes I doubt he would order for himself. This must mean he cares for me, at least a little bit. "There's a park close to the office."

He stacks the takeout containers. "I doubt it's a clothing-optional park." The office smells of curry and sex, an appealing combination. "And if you plan to set up our appointments, you should put that in our agreement."

I frown. "I thought it *was* in our agreement." I

straighten, lowering my feet to the carpet. "You said I control our appointments."

"You *do* control our appointments," Nate reassures me. "I propose the times. You have the option to turn down those times."

I relax. "Then propose the time for tomorrow at noon." I wave my hands. "What's the big freakin' deal?"

Nate's lips flatten. "The big freakin' deal is we have an agreement. If we follow that agreement we'll both know what to expect." He taps on his keyboard. "I'm busy tomorrow at noon."

"Then I guess I can *expect* to eat alone tomorrow." I can't suppress my sarcasm.

"And I have a meeting in five minutes." Nate ignores me, his focus on his screen, his expression cool and detached. "You should get dressed."

He's kicking me out of his office. "Yeah, yeah, yeah." I jump to my feet and gather my clothes, feeling very much like the hooker he's hired me to be. "You need to work on your pillow talk, Romeo."

"The women I pay don't expect pillow talk." Nate doesn't look at me, my executive now in business mode.

"Then what do you talk about after you fuck?" I yank on my skirt and the frayed fabric rips.

"We talk about payment and the next appointment." He shrugs. "They leave quickly."

"I'm not surprised," I mutter. Especially if he's as snitty with them as he is with me. "Well, I won't be leaving quickly." I button my blazer. "We're living together so you'll need to master pillow talk."

"You'll leave." The printer behind Nate hums, spewing out papers. "After we're done you'll return to your bedroom and I'll stay in mine."

I stare at him. "We have separate bedrooms?"

"Of course." Nate spreads out the papers on his desk. "That was outlined in the contract."

"You said we'd be living together," I remind him. "Sleeping in separate bedrooms isn't living together."

"I thought you wanted your freedom, Miss Trent." Nate circles a number on one of the pages. I'm now Miss Trent, a business associate, someone he doesn't want, doesn't need, doesn't care about. "Separate bedrooms will give you freedom."

I gaze at him, confused. I thought I wanted my freedom also. "But—"

"No buts." He interrupts my protest. "I've sent a copy of the contract to your private e-mail address. Read it. That's what you can expect from me. Nothing more."

He's dismissing me. No one dismisses me. I glare at him. "You can take your contract and shove it where the sun doesn't shine."

"That's very mature," Nate drawls, his cold tone escalating my anger.

"If you wanted mature you should have found yourself another hooker, preferably one sporting her natural hair color." I stomp around the office, slamming my heels down on the thick plush carpet, not ready to leave him, not yet.

"The exit is that way." He points at the door, his blond head remaining bowed over the printouts.

"I'm going," I huff. "Take a good look at this ass, Iceman." I smack my rear. "Because this could be the last time you'll ever see it." I blast though the door, my head held high.

Nate doesn't stop me, doesn't say anything, because he and I both know I'm bluffing. I will see him again. The damn man has me wound up so tight, I'm a bit crazy.

Okay, I'm a whole lot of crazy. I double-time it down the hallway, irritated with him, with myself, with the entire world.

"Miss Trent," a man calls. "About your expense reports—"

"What do you want?" I yell, throwing my hands upward. The tallest corporate clone gulps and sits down.

At least someone responds to my pain. I move even faster, whipping through the reception area, and I jab the down elevator button ten times.

"It only needs to be pressed once," Gladys, the gate-keeper, advises.

I don't acknowledge her presence. If I talk to her what I say won't be nice, and she's close to a thousand years old. She might have a heart attack. Then I'll have a death on my hands and no one will take me seriously when I say I'm all about peace and love.

The elevator doors open and the space is thankfully empty. It's one o'clock. I should return to the legal floor and give Miss Yen at least one more hour of work before I mentally check out for the day.

I never do what I should. I press the button for the ground floor and drum my heels into the tile. My arrangement with Nate is proof of that. The true me never would have agreed to that contract. I signed it to make him happy, and when I did that I promised to follow his rules, to change, to become someone I'm not.

The elevator goes express, descending without stopping once. He'll try to hold me to that promise and our fighting will escalate until our relationship finally ends. As all of my relationships have ended. With disaster, disappointment, pain.

The elevator doors open and I hightail it through the lobby. Jerome, the evil security guard, isn't at his post, and the afternoon security guard isn't giving anyone a rough time. He's slouched in his chair, his head bowed and his arms crossed, his hat tilted over his closed eyes.

I exit through the revolving doors, step into the sunshine, and release a sigh of relief. I'm free. There are no walls, no rules, no uptight CFOs I'm destined to disappoint.

I play hooky from work for an hour and a half, hiding in the park in which Nate is too busy to have lunch. A hedge divides this natural space from the rest of the world. Rows of yellow, white, and blue flowers nod in the warm summer breeze. I sit on a wooden bench under a tree, slip off my shoes and bury my toes in the green grass, savoring the connection to Mother Earth, to my hippie roots.

I need this connection. Even in my studio apartment there are herbs growing in pots along my windowsill. Will Nate allow me to keep my plants? He said he'd bring over all of the contents of my apartment. Are plants considered contents?

I shouldn't have signed that contract. I put on my shoes and trudge back to Blaine Technologies. Nate will try to enforce each and every clause in his monster contract and I'll fight him. That's my nature.

I have to find a way to sever our agreement. The sleeping security guard doesn't stir as I walk past him. My friend Kat says there are loopholes in every document. There must be a loophole in Nate's contract.

I return to the legal floor to do my remaining time. The pinch-faced lady is huffing about a phone ringing. I roll my eyes. She works in an office building. Phones ring in office buildings. Get over it, lady.

"Green," Miss Yen hollers as I near my desk.

What is it now? I smother my shriek. I can't handle any more problems today. "Yeah?" I blow into her office and plunk my ass down in the guest chair, not having the energy to be civil.

Miss Yen gives me a dirty look. "Mr. Lawford wants to speak with you. Did you resubmit the expense reports?"

Mr. Lawford can suck my big toe. "Yes, I've resubmitted the expense reports." I cross my arms. There must be a way to terminate our contract.

Miss Yen is known for negotiating contracts. That's how she landed her dragon lady nickname. She draws blood at the bargaining table.

"I made a mistake and signed a contract I shouldn't have signed," I swallow my pride and confess to my boss. "What do I do?"

She presses her lips together. "What is this contract for?"

"It's for ... ummm ..." Hot sex. Multiple orgasms. Hand jobs in the shredding room. "Services."

Miss Yen narrows her eyes. "If these *services* aren't legal the contract isn't worth the paper it is written on. Pursuing any breach of contract issues will likely result in charges being laid for all parties involved."

I chew on my bottom lip. Nate is a smart guy. He knows that. "Then why would you draft a contract you couldn't enforce?"

"This *is* something illegal." Miss Yen rubs her hands over her face. "Of course it is. Why would I expect anything else?" She gazes upward for a couple of seconds, as though seeking divine guidance from the ceiling tiles. "Some parties draft contracts to set expectations. There are no surprises with a contract. Everything is in writing."

This sounds plausible. Nate doesn't like surprises and he's always yammering about expectations. "But if they can't enforce the contract what good is it?" I ask.

"They're trusting the other party to uphold the contract."

He's trusting me to uphold the contract. All hope I have of wiggling out of this deal vanishes. I can't break Nate's trust, can't betray him. "Thank you, Miss Yen. I'll speak with Nate." I stand and smooth down my torn skirt. "Eventually."

"He prefers to be called Mr. Lawford," my boss advises. "And get a new suit, Green."

"Clothing is the least of my worries," I mutter as I return to my desk. My phone is ringing. I glance at the screen. It's Nate's number. I turn the ringer off and clip my phone to my skirt. I'll talk to him, but not now. I have to think about what I will say, about how we can save our relationship. We can't continue to fight, not for the entire month.

The wall of shredding behind me has grown, the cardboard boxes blocking the windows. I grab one box and heft it to the shredding room. The shredding has to be done and it's brain-dead work. I can think about my issues with Nate while I labor.

The machine growls as I feed it pieces of paper. I shred all of the files, flatten the box, add the cardboard to the stack, and retrieve another box.

My phone buzzes and Nate's number displays on the small screen. I admire his persistence and ignore his call, not yet ready to talk to him, having no solution for our relationship mess.

I stuff a thick file into the shredder. There might not be a solution. Nate and I might be doomed. The machine jams, grinding to a stop. I yank on the papers, peel them apart, feed them separately, my mood somber.

My phone's screen flashes red. Someone has accessed my apartment, breaking my electronic locks. I rush to my desk, type in my surveillance address, and examine the video feed on the larger monitor.

A huge rough-looking man is frantically pulling on the alarm wires. Three men stand behind him, waving their gloved hands, their mouths moving. I zoom in with the camera lens. Lawford Relocation Services is written across their navy-blue shirts in white block letters.

Lawford Relocation Services is one of the many companies owned by Nate's dad, a prominent LA real-estate developer and tough-as-nails billionaire. Nate isn't waiting for my keys or my security codes. I suck air through my front teeth. He's moving me now.

I can't truly be angry with him. He said he'd move me today, and he isn't the type of man to wait for anyone's permission. I remotely disarm the alarms and the men stop ripping at the wires.

Should I go home and supervise their efforts? I hover over the computer, undecided. My apartment isn't large and the men are working quickly, placing everything in boxes, stuffing packing popcorn around my potted plants, disconnecting my computer equipment. The bus I take to and from work doesn't run very often. The movers will be gone before I arrive.

Nate appears on the screen, looking out of place in his suit and tie. I know his schedule. He has meetings booked for the entire afternoon. What is he doing at my place? I sit down and watch him.

A mover holds up the battered pot in which I cook rice. Nate nods and the man carefully places the pot into a box. I move the view from camera to camera as Nate walks around my studio apartment. He touches my parents' framed first summer solstice photo, the rainbow-colored crocheted bedspread my mom made for me, my collection of fine leather corsets.

"Have you added breaking and entering to your long list of crimes?" I text him.

Nate reaches inside his jacket, removes his phone, glances down at the screen, and then around him. He locates the camera and types into his phone. "I agreed to move the contents of your apartment."

He's keeping his promise, potential jail time be damned. I grin, impressed. "I didn't think that meant you'd be personally involved. Don't you have meetings you should be attending?"

"You didn't answer your phone." Nate sits on my tiny bed, the mattress dipping beneath him. "Someone has to supervise the movers. Do you wish to join me?"

Yes, I wish to join him . . . on my bed. I move the camera lens, scanning my one-room apartment. The movers have stripped it bare, taking everything, including the curtains. "Nah," I type. "You appear to have everything under control. I trust you."

Nate stares down at his phone. Minutes pass. He pockets the phone and stands, his expression solemn. He opens my nightstand, the nightstand that holds my collection of black panties.

I turn off my screen, unable to watch Nate snoop through my things. He'll know all of my secrets before the move is completed. I grab a random stack of papers and take the elevator to the finance floor. If he can snoop I can also.

As I exit the elevator Gladys, Nate's gatekeeper, frowns, worry lines feathering her round face. "I've been expecting you." She dangles a set of keys from her index finger. "Return the keys to Mr. Lawford when you're done with them."

Nate is giving me permission to snoop, granting me access to his office, his filing cabinets, everything. I swallow my wonder and take the keys from Gladys, my fingers trembling. "I will. Thank you."

"He's a good man, Miss Trent, and he trusts you." She pushes her glasses upward until they are snug against the bridge of her button nose. "Don't betray his trust."

"I'll keep his secrets safe, Gladys," I vow, touched by Nate's faith in me. He won't regret this, ever. I pass over the threshold and tramp along the hallway, entering the finance department.

Today I'll open more of Nate's locked doors. I twirl his keys around one of my fingers, the clinking of metal against metal musical. I'll uncover his secrets, learn more about the man I care for.

I stride into his private space and glance around the office. Where should I start? Although the filing cabinets tempt me they're situated far away from Nate's desk. In my vast experience of snooping people keep their juicy secrets close to them.

I sit in Nate's captain's chair, the black leather smelling of his cologne, light and fresh and unmistakably masculine. My pussy moistens, my mons bare under my torn skirt. I hike up the garment and swivel my hips, grinding my scent into his seat. He'll smell me for days.

Humming happily, I unlock Nate's desk and slide open the top drawer. His fountain pen collection is impressive. All seventeen pens are black yet each one is unique and beautiful. I glide my fingertips over their smooth sleek barrels, the same barrels Nate holds in his big hands.

There's an empty space in his custom-made drawer insert. I unclip the pen from my corset and place it where it belongs, its gold nib gleaming against the black velvet. The pens clearly mean something to Nate. I can't take one away from him.

I open drawer after drawer, systematically searching his desk. All of his office supplies are the best, items not found in the main supplier's catalogue. His sticky notes are crafted from fine linen paper. His stapler is a work of art, engraved with flowing swirls. The tins holding his mints are black enamel, trimmed with gold.

He buys the best and he has bought me, quirky strange Camille Trent. I flip through the printed checks waiting for his signature. It would be easy to take one of these checks, change the name, and cash it at one of those fast money places. I frown. Nate should store them more securely.

I walk my fingers across the file folders hanging in the bottom drawer. Boring. Boring. Boring. I don't care about vendor agreements or board meeting minutes. I skip over our contract. I'm looking for something new, something juicy, something . . . like this.

I remove a massive file neatly labeled CHILD SUP-PORT PAYMENTS in block type. My heart squeezes. Does Nate have a child? I glance at the painting of the mother and child. No. I never discovered a child in all of my research and Nate, Mr. I-Need-Sole-Custody, wouldn't be an absentee dad.

I place the file on the leather desktop. The papers are yellow and brittle, the font faded. Nate's full name is printed on the header of a spreadsheet, the columns titled with Date, Description, Original Estimate, and Final Cost.

The dates start nine months before Nate was born, and every conceivable child-related cost is listed: taxi rides to doctor appointments, late-night gourmet food cravings, a pack of gum to disguise the smell of his mom's morning sickness. No item is too small, too insignificant, too overpriced.

The original estimates are outrageous and the final costs double or triple those estimates. I shake my head. Rich folks have some crazy ideas about what a child needs. Growing up on a commune, I never wore thousand-dollar baby booties. I stare at the prices, disbelieving my eyes. But somehow I survived.

I lean back in Nate's chair and continue to read, the multipage spreadsheet telling the story of his life from his conception to his eighteenth birthday. Any event, any change that requires money is detailed, including five paternity tests.

I can understand asking for one paternity test. While I was growing up I often wished my dad would ask for one. I knew he'd love me whether I was biologically his or someone else's, and having another dad would have explained why I'm so different. Maybe there's a green-haired former hippie sitting in front of a computer somewhere.

Nate's dad, being a billionaire, would have more reasons to ask for a paternity test. I watch the news. I see how baby mamas come out of the woodwork whenever a man becomes rich and famous.

Asking for five tests seems a bit excessive, though, veering from the realm of helpful and informative into hurtful and vindictive.

The other Nate-related expenses are more innocuous. They include a parade of around-the-clock-care nannies, candles for his birthday cakes, the braces he needed as a preteen, his private-school tuition, the brand-new Mercedes given to him when he turned sixteen, summers in Europe, and a Harvard education. Even the silver Rolex Nate wears is listed, a graduation present given to him by his mom, the expense reimbursed by his dad.

Why would anyone track this information? I toss the papers onto his desk. And why does Nate keep this summary? Does he think this is his worth, that all of these monetary expenses represent who he is or how much he is loved? Is this why he buys love, paying for sex?

I walk to the windows and stare at the darkening sky. Nate left his keys for me. He knows I'll find this file.

He believes I can help him.

Chapter Six

WHILE WAITING FOR Nate to return, I complete my exploration of his office, finding nothing more of interest, no more clues about his family history. I then check his schedule for tomorrow.

His lunch hour *is* booked, the appointment mysterious. It has no internal attendees and is labeled with the month. This vagueness provokes my curiosity, not my jealousy. Nate is strictly a one-hooker man, preferring serial paid monogamy.

My snooping concluded, I temporarily push thoughts of Nate aside and work on my data-sharing program. The subcontractors I've hired are asking me for guidance. I'm great at fighting other people's decisions. Making them isn't my strength. I study the four website templates a guy in India designed for me.

The door opens and the tiny hairs on the back of my neck stand to attention. Nate's scent intensifies.

"Good. You're here." I frown, suppressing the urge to run to him, to throw myself into his arms, to tell him he's greater than the dollars in his bank account. "Tell me which one of these you like." I turn the screen toward him.

"Consulting on your projects isn't in our agreement." Nate saunters closer, appearing cool, unapproachable, perfect. "And why are three of my best analysts processing the legal department's expense reports?"

I ignore his question. "Kissing isn't in our agreement either. Stop following your rules for one freakin' moment and help me choose."

Nate leans over and studies the designs, his body seductively close to mine. "If you actually read our agreement you'd know it covers kissing."

If I don't read the agreement I can break his rules and claim ignorance. "Sit," I command. Nate slides into the seat and I shimmy onto his lap, using him as my personal chair. He stiffens, his muscles flexing beneath me, his cock hardening, and I brace, waiting for him to issue a protest, to push me away. He says nothing, his attention focused on the screen.

"What are you trying to accomplish?" he asks.

"I want rich folks to either donate their unused data capacity or donate buckets of money so we can buy data capacity." I settle deeper into his physique, his form firm and deliciously warm, his pants-covered erection pressing against my ass cheeks. "I figure you'll know what appeals to rich folks. You're loaded."

"I know being referred to as *loaded* doesn't appeal

to them," Nate states dryly. He splays the fingers of his left hand over my stomach, stopping my wiggling. "Mrs. Blaine told me you're starting a business together."

"Mrs. Blaine has baby brain big-time." I roll my eyes, very much aware of him, his scent, his breath, his touch. "She's not starting anything. And business is so ... so materialistic. This is better. This could change the world."

Nate says nothing, enlarging one of the images.

"Because if we're not careful," I continue, "the mobile revolution could be used to oppress the less fortunate. Sure, the ruling elite gives money-challenged individuals their obsolete phones, presenting the image that access is available to all, but that is simply an illusion." I warm to my topic, my body vibrating with excitement. "Without voice and data plans, the phones are useless. This impending disaster is similar to the way we gave third-world countries computer equipment when they didn't have the infrastructure to operate them."

"If I recall correctly humanity survived the computer equipment disaster." Nate rests his chin on my shoulder. "This is the best of the four." He taps on the screen. "Change the font and the stock photo and it's workable."

"Awesome tips, lover." I check the box for that image, add his notes to the comment section, and send it back to the designer.

"We're not lovers," Nate points out. "We have a business arrangement. Don't get any ideas, Miss Trent."

"I guess I should call off the wedding, then. Mom

and Dad will be disappointed," I tease. Nate frowns, his breath blowing against my ear. "That's a joke, Mr. Serious," I clarify. "You don't have to worry about shotgun weddings. My parents aren't even married."

"I'm aware of your parents' marital status."

He knows a lot about me for someone in a business arrangement. I open my next e-mail. A different subcontractor asks which payment alternatives we'll accept. "Ugh. There are so many decisions."

"Decisions come with running any organization." Nate checks all of the options.

I send this answer to the subcontractor, turn my head, and kiss Nate on his square chin, showing my gratitude physically. He stares at me, his body suddenly still, his confusion palpable.

"We aren't fucking," he bluntly states. "I have work to do."

I raise an eyebrow. Does he think kissing always leads to fucking? "You're right. We aren't fucking. We're kissing." I capture his face between my hands and slant my lips over his. Nate doesn't open to me, and I prod the seam of his lips with my tongue, striking again and again and again, plunging deeper into his heat.

He sighs and concedes defeat, parting his lips. I surge inside, hitting him hard and fast, bombarding my executive with my passion, thoroughly kissing him, leaving no inch of his mouth unconquered. His chest heaves against me, his tongue entwining with mine.

This is my signal to retreat. I withdraw as quickly as I advanced, returning my attention to my overflowing e-mail box, acting as though nothing has happened, showing him we can kiss and not do more.

"What was that all about?" he demands.

"That was a kissing break." I scan my e-mail inbox. "What should we work on next?"

"*We* are not working on anything, Miss Trent." Nate eases me off his lap. "I pay you. We have sex. That's the end of our relationship. No kissing breaks, no helping with other projects, and no changing expectations."

He's setting more rules. I fume, my temper flaring. He knows rules drive me ballistic. He knows I'll storm off and leave him alone. That is what he wants me to do.

He won't trick me this time. I force myself to remain calm, to stand next to his chair, to not leave his side. "Thank you for supervising the movers." I stroke across the breadth of his shoulders, brushing my fingertips over him, back and forth, back and forth.

Nate leans into my touch, his body hungry for what his lips won't ask for. "You're never returning there." He scowls. "Ever. It isn't safe." He opens a drawer, removes the unsigned checks, and plunks them on the desktop. "That apartment building is a potential crime scene, and one of the next victims could be you."

"Would you care if I was the next victim?" I swirl my fingers into his muscles. His body is firm, his tension tangible.

"You're not setting one foot inside that building." Nate doesn't answer my question. "You deserve better, the best."

"You deserve happiness and love." I press my lips to

his nape and his shoulders shudder. "That's my definition of the best."

He gazes down at the first check, not moving, not saying anything, his forehead furrowed. It's a simple vendor payment, unworthy of this serious consideration.

"Spit it out, Nate," I urge, pushing him as I always do. "Say what you want to say."

"I'm working." He cradles the fountain pen I returned to him in his fingers. It is one of the most expensive pens an executive can buy. "You can show yourself out."

I pressed him too hard and he's dismissing me. Again. "I don't think so." I remove my jacket and drop it on the carpet. Nate doesn't look up, his blond head bent over the checks. "I'm keeping you company, lover."

"We're not lovers." He sets one check to the side. "And I don't need company."

"You don't know what you need." I walk toward the windows, unzipping my skirt as I move, uncaring that the door is open, that any of Nate's employees could walk in, see me half-naked. My skirt falls to the floor.

The nib of the pen rasps against the paper faster and faster. I unfasten my leather corset, loosening the laces hook by hook.

The door clicks closed. "I don't have time for sex," he bluntly states.

"I'm not offering you sex, Romeo. I'm thinking." I grip the window frame and spread my legs. "I do my best thinking naked. Freeing the body frees the mind." I glance over my shoulder. "You should try it sometime."

"My mind is too damn free around you." Nate stares

at me, his gaze fixed on my back. "I knew you'd have one." His voice is low.

Does he like it? "It's my only permanent tattoo." The green ivy creeps up my back, the two entwining vines thin and fine and delicate, the color matching my hair.

The temporary tattoos I wore in the past were changed to shock and appall, public works of art designed for whatever audience I wished to warn away from me. This permanent tattoo is an expression of my inner self and is completely concealed by the corsets I wear, kept private. Very few people have seen it.

I don't know why I'm showing it to Nate. "It's a reminder of our connection to the earth."

I turn, and his gaze shifts to my stomach. A tiny green stone gleams in my belly button. "It's not an emerald if that's what you're thinking." I flick it, and reflected rays of light dance across the carpet. "I doubt it has any value." I slide my hands upward and cup my breasts, my nipples tightening. "It certainly isn't *the best*."

I wait for him to say something, anything. Moments pass. Fear of his disapproval flows into anger, defiance. He doesn't like it? Fine. I don't care about his opinion.

"You've removed your other body jewelry," he finally states, his tone flat.

I however hear the judgment I always expect to hear. "Well, I'm not removing this piece of body jewelry." I glare at him. "I'm not becoming whoever you think I should be, Nate. I can't conform."

He opens his mouth.

"And don't try to use the contract to control me." I

stop him. "I'm here because I want to be here, not because of words on a paper."

"If you *read* the contract," Nate's eyes cool to a frigid pale gray, the temperature in the office dropping a couple of degrees, "you'd know you could wear as much body jewelry as you wish." He returns to his chair, sitting down behind his massive desk. "And I don't need you here. I have work to do."

"You might not need me here," I retort, "but you want me here. That's why you gave me your keys." He doesn't look at me, his lack of attention driving me crazy. "Don't let my presence stop you from completing your precious work."

I flop down on the floor, the carpet immaculately clean and sinfully soft against my bare skin. Nate taps on his keyboard, his keystrokes forceful and fast. I stare up at the ceiling and count the gray specks in the white surface, gradually calming.

He didn't ask me to remove my body jewelry. He didn't suggest I cover up my tattoo. He has admitted to sucking great big hairy donkey balls at pillow talk, and I jump all over him for making an innocent observation. I groan. He'll never talk to me again.

"Everyone else asks me to change," I explain, trying to repair the damage I've caused. "I assumed you wanted me to change also." He says nothing. "And I can't change. I've tried, lord knows I've tried, but I am who I am and I refuse to be seen as less, as a disappointment because I'm different."

The silence is deafening, my executive remaining angry with me.

"Right now is a prime example." I take a deep breath, count to ten, and exhale. "You likely want me to shut up because all you desire is a sexual relationship. I thought that's what I wanted too, but I've been so lonely," I ramble on, unable to stop talking. "Anna has Mr. Blaine and Emily. Kat has Mr. Henley and the wedding to plan. My parents live on the hippie commune with a shared phone. I need to talk, and I want to talk to you for some strange reason." I frown, unsure why I want to talk to him. "But you don't have to listen if you don't want to."

Nate offers no reply.

Taking this as agreement, I close my eyes and talk. I talk about the project I'm working on, how I don't know if anyone will be interested in it. I talk about Michael, a guy I liked at my previous job. He kissed me twice in the parking lot yet wouldn't acknowledge our relationship in public, calling me a freak in front of his friends, making me feel less than I was. I talk about how I'd go to extremes with my appearance, wearing a Mohawk, body jewelry, temporary tattoos, to filter out the people who would never accept me.

My words and thoughts slow, my limbs growing heavy. I had very little sleep last night, having worked on the data donation project until the early hours of the morning. Tonight will be another late night. I have code to write and boxes to unpack and a lover to please.

"We have a business arrangement." Nate's voice finds me in the darkness. "We're not lovers."

Nate is with me, watching over me, keeping me safe. I smile and drift into the abyss.

I'M FLOATING IN the clear blue skies above one of the commune's many gardens. This plot of land is planted with thyme, basil, cilantro, and other herbs. All I smell is mint, the scent engulfing me, soothing my soul. The sun warms my body, adding to my sense of peace and tranquility. I'm safe and protected, accepted by the universe.

"Fuck," the universe curses, the sky shaking.

I open my eyes and gaze up at Nate's handsome face. His jaw is jutted, his cheekbones defined, his tanned skin shadowed. He's clad in his shirt, his black tie loosened. I'm wearing his jacket and his arms are wrapped around me tightly. "You're carrying me," I state the obvious.

"You sleep like the dead," he grumbles, crimson creeping up his neck.

"The commune had shared accommodations." The other girls I shared a dorm with were homeschooled and would take turns trying to keep me awake, seeking to sabotage my attempts to connect with the outside world, to force me to become who they wanted me to be. I refused to conform, stubborn and stuck in my deviant ways even as a child.

Nate carries me down a hallway. The walls are painted a classic white. The black furniture and fixtures are simple and tasteful and very expensive, the best of everything. Black and white works of art hang on the wall. There are no personal photos, no color, no chaos; every item is in its rightful spot. "This must be your home."

He says nothing, walking purposefully, his grip on my near-naked body secure. I'm awake. There's no reason for Nate to continue carrying me unless he wants to hold me.

I want him to hold me. I want him. I flatten my right palm against his chest. His heart beats under my fingertips, strong and reliable and true. "Why am I wearing your jacket?" His cotton shirt is delectably soft.

The flush moves to Nate's chin. "Your suit disintegrated when I tried to dress you."

He tried to dress me, to take care of me. "I guess I'm going to work naked tomorrow, then." I smile at him, too drowsy to be concerned. "Miss Yen won't like that."

"There are suits in your closet." Nate pushes a door open with his right shoulder. "You could choose one of those to wear."

I could *choose* to wear something I wouldn't normally wear, to change for him. "Okay." It would only be for one day, and I don't have any other options. Blaine Technologies' has a very strict dress code. Nudity is frowned upon.

We enter a huge bedroom and my jaw drops. The furniture and hardwood floor are black, matching the rest of the house. The walls, curtains, and throw rug are an unexpected green, the same color as my hair. My mom's rainbow-colored bedspread partially covers the massive bed, bright and happy and familiar. "You have color in your home."

"This is your room." Nate's voice is gruff. He carefully sets me down on the bed. "Your clothes are folded in the dressers. The contents of your bathroom are in there." He waves at the brightly lit connected space. "The things I couldn't place remain in boxes downstairs. Arrange them wherever you want." He steps backward.

The things *he* couldn't place. He personally arranged my things. I hook my fingers around Nate's belt, holding onto him, preventing his retreat. "Where did you put my herbs?"

"If you're talking about the plants the gardener set them on the kitchen windowsill." Nate's spine is straight, his form rigid and unyielding, his expression stern.

He has a gardener and a kitchen with a windowsill. My gaze lowers. And a hard-on, the ridge in his dress pants pronounced and undeniable. "Everything is taken care of." I rub one of my hands over him, savoring his size, his energy. "Everything except this."

Nate watches me hungrily, his need reflected in his pale gray eyes, his body swaying into my palm. "I'm tired, Camille."

He *must* be tired. He called me by my first name. "Then come here." I pull back the bedspread and pat the sheets, the white fabric silky smooth, the best. "Let me take care of you."

His fingers fold into tight fists.

"Ah . . . but I forgot." I unbutton his shirt, revealing tanned skin and defined muscle. He's perfect and mine. For now. I push the cotton off his shoulders and his shirt drifts to the floor, a white billowing cloud covering a field of green carpet.

"I'm supposed to allow you to set our appointments."

I trail my lips down his chest, tasting the salt of his skin, and he shudders, his shoulders shaking, his eyes darkening. Every inch of him is sculpted and hard.

"But I never do anything I'm supposed to do." I unbuckle his belt, unzip his pants, release him, and stroke him, enjoying his pure maleness. He's less crisp here, less proper, his musk mixing with the mint scent. I inhale deeply, imprinting him on my brain.

His thighs tremble. I gaze up at him, my lips pursed a breath away from his tip. He's exhausted, shadows framing his eyes.

"Lie down, Nate," I order, my voice as firm as my grip. His lips part. "This is nonnegotiable," I add, my man deliciously stubborn. He would never change simply to fit in, to be loved. Nate is Nate.

He sits on the bed, the mattress dipping under his weight, and he lies down, resting his golden head on the white pillow. A soul-deep sigh escapes his lips.

"You don't know what you need." I remove his shoes and socks, lift his big finely groomed feet to the bed. "But I do."

He folds his arms behind his head, his naked body displayed for me, his cock proudly erect. Nate is no longer the Iceman, cold and unattainable. He's my glorious human man, tired and aroused, needing comfort and relief.

"I know what I need also." I toss his jacket off my shoulders, my body as naked as his, and his cock bobs, his appreciation precious and pure, unsullied by words. "Since I first saw you standing in the elevator, clad in your perfect black suit, I've wanted to do this." I drag my breasts along his firm physique, massaging his muscles with my nipples, the slide of skin over skin erotic, real, breathtakingly intimate.

Nate shakes under me, his biceps bulging. He doesn't hold me, doesn't touch me, allowing me to explore every dip, every swell, every inch of him.

I kiss and lick and suck, watching his reactions, learning what he likes. His flat male nipples are especially sensitive. I circle them with my fingernails, teasing him into a sexual frenzy.

"Camille." Nate pushes his hips upward, sliding his shaft between my thighs. I move lower, spreading my legs, and my pussy lips connect with his hot flesh. He rocks as I play with his right nipple, nipping, tugging, laving him with my tongue.

I focus on him, showing him everything I can't say, everything he isn't ready to hear, might never be ready to hear, my link to him, this impossible broken man, as deep and as true as my connection to the earth.

This link between us, this change within me, is permanent. I will never be the same. I glide down his body, licking a path to Nirvana. His body stills, tenses, his eyes widening. A bead of pre-cum forms on his tip.

"Kissing is covered by our contract, right?" I smile at him.

Nate stares at me, his gaze thunderous with desire. I extend my tongue and electricity surges around us, the air crackling as it does before a summer storm. Holding both his gaze and his shaft, I flick his tip.

"Camille," he cries, his body bowing, lightning flashing in his eyes.

"Easy, lover," I purr. "I didn't give you permission to come." I clasp the base of his cock harder, assisting him with his control. "You'll find release when I squeeze your balls." I bend over him and nuzzle them. His toes curl. "And not a moment sooner." I suck on his sensitive skin and he kicks his feet. "I'm in control now." I lick his slightly curved shaft, following a pulsing vein. Nate's lips flatten.

This powerful man's satisfaction rests in my hands and between my lips. I twirl my tongue around his tip and dip into his slit, savoring his essence, Nate's flavor as unique as he is. His chest rises and falls, his muscles flexing beneath me.

"You're my lover, Nate," I murmur against his skin. "Words on a paper and money in the bank won't alter this truth." I push my lips over his tip and suck. He groans, lifting his ass off the mattress.

I take him deeper into my mouth. Taking all of him is impossible. He's too large and I'm no porn star. His cock head taps the back of my throat. I wrap my fingers around his remaining shaft and I inhale, tugging on his flesh.

A strangled noise comes from Nate's throat, his eyes wild, his hands clenching behind his head. I release and he relaxes. I suck again. He tenses and I chuckle, the sound muffled by the huge cock in my mouth.

He's easy to torture. I bob up and down him, varying my pressure, intent on driving him absolutely crazy.

"Camille." His voice cracks.

I release him with a juicy pop. "Who am I to you, Nate?" I brush my fingertips over his balls, reminding him that he can't come until I squeeze them. "Am I merely some random hooker you've hired to take care of your needs?"

He presses his lips together mulishly. He knows what I want to hear.

"Fine. Be that way." I bend over him once more and suck him deep, fluttering my tongue against his shaft. His thighs shake and his breathing grows harsh.

"No," Nate growls. "You're more."

I smile around his cock. He cares for me. I roll his balls with my fingers as I fuck him with my mouth, drawing my lips along his cock.

"I said the words," Nate states, the sexual strain written on his face, lines creasing his golden skin. "Give me release."

Nate and his agreements. I sink down on him, cup his balls, and squeeze.

"Camille," he roars, driving his hips upward. I move with him, riding his bucking body, his release violently strong. His hot cum shoots down my throat, filling my mouth, coating my tongue. I swallow and suck, swallow and suck, draining him dry, not wasting a single drop, my cheeks indenting around him.

Nate thrusts once more, shudders, and collapses, his body relaxing and his breath leveling. "You're everything." His voice is drowsy.

I lap the flat of my tongue over him, cleaning him,

caring for him. He doesn't move, doesn't say anything more. I peer up at him. His eyes are closed and his handsome face is softened by sleep.

Yes, my heart will definitely break at the end of this month. "I'll take care of you, Nate," I whisper, holding him tight. "You're my everything also."

Chapter Seven

I WAKE IN a dimly lit room and reach for Nate. My fingers touch cotton. I'm alone. There's an indentation in the pillow where his head has been, the decadently soft bedsheets are pulled over my naked body, and the light in the bathroom has been turned on.

I might mean more than a sexual release to him, but I'm not much more, not yet. I hug the pillow to my chest, inhaling his scent. We have a month. His feelings could change in a month.

My new bedroom is massive, bigger than my entire apartment. The walls are covered with striped fabric, one shade of green slightly darker than the other. Three of my mom's oil paintings hang in the room, the landscapes cheerful and happy.

The crystals in the light fixture above me sparkle. Three dressers guard the perimeter. The photo of my mom and dad has been placed on a nightstand, beside my company passcard. A wooden writing desk is positioned in front of the window, one of my computers set on its surface.

I bounce out of the bed, my toes sinking into the lush carpet, and stride toward the desk. The view is fantastic. The moon and stars shine in the dark sky, illuminating grass, a swimming pool, flowers.

I start up my computer and sit down on a delicate wooden chair, the silky soft seat cushioning my bare ass. The house is quiet as I focus on my data-sharing project: answering e-mails, adding lines of codes, making dreaded decisions.

I work until the sun rises and the birds sing. Then I saunter into the bathroom. My ratty old towels look out of place against the sparkling white tile and silver fixtures. My toothbrush hangs in the holder. My brush rests on the counter. My birth-control pills are hidden in the medicine cabinet. My shampoo and conditioner have been placed in the shower stall.

I quickly complete my morning routine. In the past getting prepped took hours, as I had to put my hair into a Mohawk, touch up my temporary tattoos, insert all of the hardware, filling the holes in my ears, tongue, lip. Conforming saves time.

My panties are stored neatly in the top drawer of a dresser. Nate had painstakingly folded each dainty scrap of lace. And he must have been responsible for their care. I grin as I don a pair. I can't imagine the rough tough moving men being this conscientious with my intimate garments.

I open the closet. It's as big as the bathroom, a light shining on the gleaming wood floor. My inappropriate-for-work, rave-worthy dress hangs in one corner, beside my collection of corsets. I spot a gorgeous green evening gown and five black leather suits in varying styles.

There are no other outfits in the cedar-scented space. I frown. Nate said I could wear one of the suits in the closet to work. He must have been referring to the leather suits.

I run my fingers over my choices. Each suit is a work of art, unique and different, garments I'd choose for myself if I had the inclination to shop.

My wonder grows as I dress. The first suit fits as though it was custom made for my body, hugging my curves and cupping my breasts. The jacket is formfitting and delectably soft. The equally tight skirt is midcalf length, the kick pleat playful and sexy.

I twirl in front of a mirror, gazing at myself from varying angles. Damn, I look badass, feminine yet strong, edgy yet conservative enough for Blaine Technologies' stodgy fashion police.

I slip on my battered heels, clip my phone and passcard to the waistband, and skip into the hallway. All of the other doors are closed and I'm tempted to explore.

My hunger is greater than my curiosity. I descend the stairs, seeking the kitchen. There's no mistaking whose house I'm now living in. Nate's clean, minimalistic, black-and-white style is reflected in every corner of the structure.

After a couple of wrong turns I locate the kitchen. I don't locate Nate. My man is missing and I'm starving.

I look in the fridge. My groceries and not much else occupy the immaculately clean shelves. I gather eggs, a green pepper, a tomato, and a block of cheddar cheese. The herbs are carefully arranged on the windowsill. I pinch the tops off some of the chive plants. My dented, darkened frying pan is stored in a bottom cupboard. The other pans appear too shiny to have ever been used.

I smile. Nate has the best of everything—a huge black-and-white kitchen, a massive center island, a beautiful black range—and he doesn't cook.

He *does* have faultless timing, though. As I'm belting out the lyrics to a very vulgar hip-hop song and sliding the second omelet onto a white china plate, my senses sound an alarm. I glance upward and stop my singing and dancing.

Nate is watching me, his big body leaning against the wall, thought lines furrowing his forehead. He's dressed as he always is, in a black suit, a white shirt, and a black tie, and his hair is wet, moisture darkening the gold strands.

"Your breakfast is ready, lover." I place a plate with an omelet at the end of the kitchen table, giving him the power seat. "I hope you like eggs and orange juice. That's all I had."

"The agreement is I pay for meals." He frowns.

Nate and his agreements. I roll my eyes. "Don't get your boxer briefs tied into a knot. We'll go grocery shopping tonight and you can pay the bill." I carry my plate to the table. It is set with dishes I suspect he's never used.

Nate doesn't move. "I normally eat out or order in."

"There's nothing normal about that," I mutter. "Sit down and eat your eggs before they get cold." Freakin' hell. I sound like my mom. I splatter hot sauce over my omelet. "Starting tonight I'll cook all of your meals."

"You're changing our agreement." Nate sits down and gazes at his omelet, his expression grim. "I knew this would happen. You'll expect more from me. Your daily rate—"

"My daily rate won't change," I assure him. This is about more than money. Money can't cause the pain I see reflected in his eyes. "I'm cooking for you because I want to, because it gives me pleasure. I don't expect anything more from you."

"You're cooking for me and you don't want anything more from me?" Nate glances toward me and I nod, biting back a sarcastic "Just eat your damn eggs already."

Silence stretches between us.

"This is a hippie thing," he finally concludes and grasps his fork.

"Wait." I stop him. "Close your eyes." He looks at me as though I'm insane. "Just do it, Mr. Suspicious." He complies. I break off a piece of his omelet with my fork. "Open your mouth." He parts his lips, and I carefully transfer a forkful of egg into his mouth. "Now tell me if you taste it."

Nate chews slowly and swallows. "Taste what?"

The love, I almost reply. This will freak my emotionally repressed man completely out. "My special ingredient," I say instead.

"What is your special ingredient?" He pokes the omelet with the tongs of his fork. "Will it cause me to fail a drug test?"

I laugh. "No. I haven't done drugs in a very long time and I certainly don't need them when I'm with you. You make me happy."

We eat breakfast. I chatter about the meals I plan to make for him, the groceries we need, and other nonsense. Nate dines quietly, devouring every morsel of his omelet, his back straight, his table manners impeccable.

After he finishes his food he sets down his fork and stares at his empty plate. I stop talking, waiting for him to share whatever is clearly bothering him. Lines appear around his eyes and mouth.

"Do I?" he finally asks.

"Do you what?" I don't know what he's referring to.

"Do I make you happy?" Nate's gaze meets mine. He's heartbreakingly serious. "Am I enough for you?"

He doesn't ask if *this* is enough for me. He asks if *he's* enough for me.

I leave my seat and climb onto his lap, and Nate stiffens. "Are we having another one of your kissing breaks?" He frowns. "Because we don't have time for sex. I have a meeting at eight o'clock."

"Relax." I smile at my stern somber man. "This *is* a kissing break." I touch his handsome face, stroking my fingers along his jaw, over his square chin. He follows my hand, nuzzling against my fingertips, seeking more contact.

"And you're enough for any woman, Nathan Lawford." I cover his lips with mine, kissing him with all of the passion in my wild soul. He hesitates for five long seconds, and then he opens to me. Our tongues dance, teasing, twisting. He tastes of breakfast and mint, always mint. I will forever associate this taste, this smell with Nate.

I smooth his eyebrows, caress his cheeks, pet his neck, giving him the touch I know he craves yet will never ask for. Nate draws me closer to his hard hot body and he sucks, tugs, nips on my lips, his exploration unhurried and thorough. Time slows, the world stopping for this, for us.

Nate releases my lips and leans his forehead against mine, his breath blowing softly on my skin. "You're not any woman." He isn't looking at my green hair or my piercings as he says this. He's looking at me.

My heart warms.

I TAKE ADVANTAGE of our commute to ask Nate's opinion on the zillions of decisions I have left to make. He wears his usual icy expression as he drives his black sedan, only his eyes reflecting his joy. I open all of the windows and his happiness increases, his lips lifting into that small smile I've grown to love.

To love. I nibble on my bottom lip. I seem to be using this word a lot around him. A cautious girl would try for some distance, attempt to cool down our relationship, protect her heart.

I'm not a cautious girl. "I'm thinking about buying tandoori chicken for lunch." This is a meal I can't make for myself, as I lack the oven. "Will you be fed in your mysterious noon meeting?"

"I should be fed." Nate's lips flatten, his countenance darkening.

"That sucky of a meeting, huh?" I rest my palm on his thigh. "Can't you blow it off?"

He drives the car into Blaine Technologies' underground parking lot, the overhead lights casting interesting shadows over his face. "Blowing off appointments with my mother has a price."

He's meeting his mom. This explains why I'm not invited to lunch. I'm not the type of woman any man introduces to his parents.

"What do you mean by 'it has a price'?" I force a laugh. "Does she send you an invoice?"

"Yes." Nate's grip on the steering wheel tightens, his knuckles whitening.

I stare at him. He's serious. His mom sends him an invoice. "If you ever ditched a meeting with my mom, she'd tell you off, and you do *not* want to experience that. Trust me."

"You told me off and I survived." Nate's gaze flicks to my face and then returns to the road.

"My mom is *much* louder." I widen my eyes dramatically. "And she wraps her arms around you, giving you a hug that's not really a hug but more like an attempted strangulation." I grin, having survived many such hugs in the past.

"My mother doesn't yell and she certainly doesn't hug." Nate slows the car, coasting the vehicle into a parking spot. A limousine dominates one corner of the floor. Two black sedans and a silver Jaguar are also parked in the predominantly gray space. "She chooses not to speak to me . . . for months."

And this bothers him. I place my left palm on my lonely executive's upper thigh. "She might not speak to you, but she can't stop you from speaking to her. Eventually you'll wear her down."

"As you wear me down." He covers my hand with his.

"Exactly." I beam, squeezing his leg. "I'll carry my phone. If you need any more tips call me." I flounce out of his car. He won't call me during his lunch with his mom, but he'll be thinking of me. I stalk toward the bank of elevators.

"What should I talk about?" Nate matches my shorter stride.

My fiercely independent man is asking me for advice. I glance up at him, warmed by his trust. "Is there a topic that drives your mom crazy? That she has a strong opinion about?"

"My father." Nate frowns. "But that topic will have a price tag associated with it." He bumps his body against my arm.

I slide my hand into Nate's larger palm. He folds his fingers over mine, gripping me tightly. "No, you shouldn't talk about your dad," I agree. "The topic should be general, like politics or fashion or celebrity marriages." I pause, rethinking this suggestion. "Well, maybe not marriages."

"That topic will cost me money also." Nate's lips twitch.

Everything costs Nate money. We stand in front of the elevator doors, holding hands, our images reflected in the mirrored surface. Neither of us pushes the button.

Nate shifts his weight from one foot to the other. "If you attend this lunch with me I'll double your fees for this week."

I gaze at him, stunned by his offer. "You want me to meet your mom?"

Nate winces. "I know dealing with my parents isn't in our agreement, but . . ."

But he wants me to attend. Being the rebel I am, I need to hear the words he won't say. "You don't have to pay me. Finish your sentence and I'll say yes."

My stubborn man remains silent, his jaw jutted.

"If you don't say the words I'll make other plans for lunch." I push him as I always do, wanting more, wanting everything.

Nate widens his stance, as though bracing for a physical attack. "I need you by my side." He lifts his chin, daring me to judge him.

He needs me. "I'd love to have lunch with you and your mom." I pat his chest, savoring his solidness. "It'll be fun."

"Appointments with my mother are never fun."

"They will be now." I swing our arms and we gaze at the closed doors, waiting for an elevator that will never come, the button remaining unpushed.

Moments pass, our connection deepening, tightening, the air around us thick and heavy with emotion. I don't move, don't speak, content to be with him, the man I suspect I love.

"Thank you." Nate finally presses the button. His expression is grim.

"I'll be on my best behavior," I promise. I won't mess this up.

His eyebrows lift. "Have I ever seen this best behavior of yours?"

I roll my eyes. "At the last quarterly meeting I was well behaved." The doors open and we step inside, our fingers remaining linked.

"That's because you were ill." He selects our floors.

I had been ill. I smile, thrilled he'd noticed. The red digital numbers change. Our images reflect on the mirrored walls. My green hair is loose, framing my face, and the black leather suit hugs my body, accentuating my pale skin. The overhead lights shine on Nate's blond hair, his tan golden, his gaze fixed on me, his eyes dark with emotion.

I slide in front of him, take his wrists, and draw his arms over my chest, wrapping them around me. "Hold me, lover."

Nate obeys my command, pulling me into his physique and clutching me tightly, resting his chin on my shoulder. He's no longer the unapproachable Iceman, and I'm not the defiant rebel child. We're a couple: real, imperfect, right.

"I have an important meeting." His chest rubs against my shoulder blades.

"I know." I suspect I know Nate's schedule better than he does. "I have coding on the data-sharing project to complete." I wiggle my ass and he groans. "We'll find the time to touch later."

"We *do* have a month." His voice is quiet.

"We have a month." The elevator doors open and I don't move, not wanting to leave him, to spend one second of our remaining time apart.

Nate releases me. "This is your floor." He places one of his palms on my back and pushes gently, propelling me into motion.

I walk away from him, not looking back, knowing if I do I'll run to him, cling to him, forgo the independence I've always valued. The office buzzes with quiet conversations.

I pass the low-talking brunette assistant from four rows down. She gazes expectantly at me, her lips parted and her brown eyes bright. Determined to behave, to fit in for once in my life, I skip my usual morning greeting and say the expected nothing. Her eyes dim and her mouth closes.

She acts as though I've disappointed her by conforming, by following the department's unspoken rules. Confused, I march toward my desk, slamming my heels against the floor.

"Green," Miss Yen hollers.

I change direction, enter my boss' office, and claim the nearest guest chair. "Intern Green reporting for duty." I salute her.

"Can the sarcasm." Miss Yen stands behind her desk, clad in a black suit, her hair twisted into a knot at the base of her neck.

"As you know there is a strict rule about working on personal projects during company time." She doesn't look at me. "If an employee is caught working on a personal project, she can be dismissed immediately." Her lips flatten.

Freakin' hell. I tense. Someone ratted me out. "I can explain."

"Don't explain anything." Miss Yen holds up one of her hands. "Let me finish." I close my mouth. "We also have a mountain of files to shred."

I groan. She's locking me in the shredding room, taking away my Internet access. This is worse than being fired. I won't be able to answer e-mail questions about my project or add any lines of code.

"In order to use the full capabilities of the new high-tech shredding machine we've ordered, Mr. Henley has boosted the connectivity in the room." Miss Yen lowers her size-zero ass into her black captain's chair.

I frown, confused. My tight-lipped boss doesn't share unnecessary information. Why is she talking about the room's connectivity?

Does she want me to use that connectivity? I stare at her.

"The machine will arrive next month," Miss Yen adds. "And you are to spend all of your time until then in the shredding room. This is your sole project, do you understand?"

I tilt my head to one side, unsure whether I do understand. It sounds as though she's telling me to hide in the shredding room, to complete my stealth coding there. "Are you saying I can work on my—"

"I'm saying nothing more," Miss Yen snaps. "Gather up your things and move into the shredding room. I don't want to see you at your desk."

I stand and smooth down my leather skirt, my thoughts spinning. Is she giving me permission to work on my project full-time? "I—"

"Don't make me repeat myself, Green." My boss' beautiful face hardens. "I've spent enough of my valuable time on this issue. I'm expecting results."

She's expecting my project to be successful. Warmth fills my soul. Miss Yen has invested her limited time arranging this opportunity. She believes in me. "Thank you, Miss Yen."

"Thank me by doing some work for a change." My boss turns toward her computer screen, dismissing me.

Chapter Eight

FOUR HOURS LATER Nate leans against the door frame of my new office, his arms crossed, his expression cool and contained. "The view in here has improved."

"Ha." I'm draped over my desk, my leather-clad ass in the air, as I plug in my phone charger. "I'm still working out the bugs." I straighten. "But what do you think?" I glance around myself with pride.

The desk, chair, computer equipment, and other office essentials were already in the room when I arrived, their existence erasing any lingering doubts I had about Miss Yen's intentions. I arranged the makeshift office quickly and dedicated the rest of the morning to my project, openly answering my phone and replying to e-mails, no longer worrying about anyone overhearing me.

"I think you need one of these." Nate places a green fountain pen on my desk. None of his pens had been green. My chest warms. He bought this gift especially for me.

"It's beautiful, lover." I skim my fingers over its barrel. The gold nib is exquisite and the engraving is fine. "Thank you."

"The person with the pen holds all of the power." He gazes across the small space, his eyes unfocused and his lips flat.

"A pen signs checks," I add quietly, now understanding their significance. He collected eighteen pens representing the eighteen years his dad paid child support, having control over him, over his mom.

Nate nods.

"I'm keeping the pen, I'll always treasure it, but I'm returning the power. Power isn't a hippie need." I press my body against his, regaining my solemn executive's attention. "We're all about love, peace, and freedom." I swivel my hips, teasing him. "Be free with me, Nate. Cast your material things aside." I throw my hands back and fall.

He hooks his arms around my waist, catching me. "You're crazy." He gives me one of his small smiles. "And we're late for lunch."

"Yes, lunch." I straighten. "I'm starving."

"You're always starving." His eyes glint.

"I have a healthy appetite . . . for everything." I hold Nate's hand as we walk down the hallway. My coworkers stare at us, the whispers swelling in waves of sound, gossip spreading. I don't care. I have a parent to meet. "What will you do if your mom doesn't like me?"

We enter the elevator. "She won't like you." There's zero doubt in Nate's voice.

"What?" I blink, temporarily stunned speechless by

his honesty. "Why? Because I have green hair, multiple piercings, don't fit into her white-bread-eating world? She can suck my—"

"She doesn't like anyone," he adds.

"Oh." My righteous rage oozes from my bones and I frown. "Your mom has to like someone. She loves you, doesn't she?"

Nate says nothing, his face darkening.

"She wouldn't have lunch with you if she didn't love you." I move closer to him, brushing against his body.

"These lunches have a price." His voice is soft.

He pays his mom to see him? I tilt back my head and gaze up at him, not hiding my disbelief. Nate reaches into his jacket and shows me a thick white business envelope.

I squeeze his hand. "You're paying me also, but that doesn't mean I don't care about you. Money has no bearing on emotions."

"It has no bearing on *your* emotions. You're a hippie." Nate's eyes glitter. "Not everyone grows their own herbs and wears the same suit until the fabric dissolves." His smile returns.

I narrow my eyes. "Are you mocking me?"

"No way, man."

I swallow my laughter, captivated by this playful side of my serious executive. "Do you want me to tell you off? Because I will and it won't be pretty. I know some foul words."

"I realize that." He chuckles. "I heard your singing this morning." The elevator doors open, and Nate leads me into the underground parking lot. The stagnant air smells of exhaust fumes and Mother Earth's tears. "I enjoyed the dancing also. I'd pay money to see that." He opens his car's passenger door.

"There's no need to pay more money." I sit down. "The singing and dancing and telling off are free, part of the many services I offer."

He shuts the door between us, moves to the driver's side, fills the sedan with his big body and crisp clean scent. "Don't ever change, Camille."

"I don't plan to change." I gaze at him, his casual comment tugging at my heart, making me want to believe in him, in us, in tomorrow.

I can't believe. Our contract only lasts a month. I can't ever forget that.

Nate drives with a grim determination, as though he's trekking into battle, his shoulders stiff and his back straight. The houses become bigger, the streets cleaner and better maintained, the colors brighter.

"Don't worry. Your mom will love me," I declare.

Nate's gaze slides to my face and then returns to the road. "You've set unreasonable expectations for this appointment."

"I'm not saying she'll declare her undying devotion during the entree." I laugh. "I'd settle for her simply agreeing to contact me."

"She'll disappoint you."

"You're underestimating me, Nate." I place my hand on his thigh and rub my fingertips into his muscles, massaging him, excited by this new challenge. "I've accomplished the impossible before."

"If anyone can do it you can," Nate murmurs, his faith in me buoying my spirits even more. He turns the car into a small street. Baskets of flowers line the sidewalk. Fine metalwork decorates the always-lit streetlights. Women with big hats, bigger sunglasses, and tiny dogs sit on restaurant patios, drinking coffee and talking on cell phones.

Nate parks in front of one of these hoity-toity restaurants. A doorman opens the door for me, holds out a gloved hand, helps me out of the vehicle. The neatly dressed young man lifts his gaze to my green hair. His smile doesn't flicker.

The restaurant patrons aren't as professional as the doorman. They stare at me, hiding their moving red lips behind finely manicured fingers, the sun's rays reflecting off their perfect nail polish.

I press my fingertips into my palms, concealing my blunt unpolished fingernails, not wishing to give the women anything else to mock. Nate hands his car keys and a folded bill to the valet and joins me on the sidewalk, taking one of my hands, linking our fingers together.

A beaming doorman holds the door open for us and we enter the restaurant. The tables are spaced far apart, every seat filled by men in dark suits or women in sleek fitted dresses. The tablecloths are white, the silverware gleams, and the crystal dazzles. Delicate white orchids sprout from round black pots. A tantalizing hint of spice lingers in the air, teasing my nostrils.

The restaurant is tasteful, stylish, and clearly a regular haunt of Nate's. As he guides me through the space pa-

trons and employees greet him by name and gaze specu-
latively at me.

"They think you're a rock star," he murmurs, leaning closer to me as we walk. "They're expecting a show."
He puts his arm around me, publicly claiming me as his
lunch date.

"I never do what anyone expects." I thrust back my
shoulders, pride fusing my spine. With Nate I'm not a freak,
a target of scorn. I'm a rock star, a woman to be envied.

Nate splays his fingers over my hip, his hand warming the leather, warming me, and leads me to a secluded
corner of the restaurant. The table is beautifully set for
three, the lighting low and the atmosphere romantic.

"This is very cozy," I comment. Nate holds my chair
and I grin as I sit down. "I thought we were having lunch
with your mom."

His eyes gleam. "This is the best table." Nate claims
the seat beside me, pressing his leg against mine, reestablishing our physical connection. "And my mother *will*
be joining us." He reaches inside his suit jacket as if to
seek reassurance that the envelope hasn't escaped. "I have
something she wants."

His mom wants money, her payment for spending time with him. "You have something I want also." I
slowly lower my gaze, openly admiring his broad shoulders, firm chest, big hands. "Lover." I linger over the en-
dearment, relishing each syllable.

"I'll give that to you later," Nate promises. "If you're
good." He pours white wine into my glass.

"Oh, I'm never good." I dip my finger into the liquid

and rub the rim of the glass round and round, making the crystal sing. "I'm a naughty, naughty girl." I lean toward him, speaking softer. "Don't you know that?"

"I had my suspicions." Nate drops his gaze to my lips. "You—"

He turns his head, his spine straightening. "She's here." Nate's face hardens and his expression cools. I shiver. He's the Iceman once more.

A woman's voice grows louder. Her tone is bored and her greetings are insincere. This must be Nate's mom. She knows everyone and likes no one. I fidget in my seat, eager to meet her, to face this challenge.

"Viola." Nate stands, his emotions concealed by a protective layer of ice.

Viola? I scramble to my feet. He calls his mom by her first name?

A tiny woman with Nate's golden hair and chilly demeanor traipses toward us, her painfully thin body clad in a winter-white skirt suit. My anticipation builds as she approaches. Nate's subzero super shield is thin and penetrable. His beautiful mother is cold to the bone, her blue eyes hard and brittle.

"Nathan." There's no affection in her voice. "Do we have to continue with this dreary lunch business?" She waves her gloved hands, maintaining her distance from her son. She doesn't kiss him, doesn't hug him, doesn't touch him. "I had to cancel a manicure with Frederick and he's impossible to book."

"Let me guess." I force my smile. It's game time. "He's the best."

"Of course. I only deal with the best." Nate's mom looks me up and down. Her top lip curls. "You've brought a guest with you," she addresses her son, ignoring me. "How trying."

"I know *I'm* trying," I quip, my smile becoming genuine. She's a worthy opponent. "I'm Camille, Nate's lover. Should I call you Mom?"

"No, you should not." She gazes around her. A waiter stands by the wall, his expression blank. No one else is situated near us. "Since you insist upon talking to me, my name is Viola."

Nate's eyes glitter as he pulls out her chair. My new buddy, Viola, sits primly, her back straight, her body rigid, her lips pursed with disapproval.

Nate faced this silent condemnation every day for decades. Alone. Today I'll face it with him. My goal is to eliminate it from his life forever.

I plunk my leather-clad ass down on my chair. "Hmmm ..." I tap my fingertips against the tabletop. "Are you certain your Frederick is the best?"

Viola gives me a haughty sniff, turning her shoulder slightly toward me. This must be the silent treatment Nate talks about. I struggle to contain my amusement.

"Because my buddy L'ongle claims he's the best." I splay my fingers, gazing at my short blunt fingernails. "He's always bothering me to get my nails done." Nate bumps his leg against mine, his face blank, his mask firmly in place. "He has high-profile clients. I helped him with some privacy-of-information concerns," I explain.

"You protected his information?" Nate's lips lift.

"I do that sometimes." I grin at him. "It throws folks off balance."

"And you didn't charge L'ongle for your services?" Nate pours wine into his mom's glass, choosing bottled water for himself.

"It's too much bother." I shrug. "What would I charge him? How do I cost out a customer's piece of mind? Some things like trust, beauty, love, are impossible to put a price on. Money merely debases their value."

"Careful." He chuckles. "Your hippie is showing."

Nate's mom stares at him. "Why are you laughing like a fool? She doesn't know L'ongle," she says, her tone icy. "She's a liar."

"Viola." Nate's eyes flash a warning, his voice even colder than his mom's.

"It's okay." I place my hand on his arm, seeking to calm him. "I suppose I don't truly know L'ongle. I believed him when he said he was the best, didn't I?" I glance around the table, looking for inspiration, searching for another reason why Viola might wish to call me. "I'm famished. Should we ask for menus?"

"I ordered in advance for all of us." Nate motions to the waiter. The neatly-dressed young man nods curtly and disappears through swinging doors.

"I have another appointment," his mom flatly states. "You can't expect me to sit here for an entire hour every single month."

They only spend an hour a month together and he has to bribe her to do that much. I rub Nate's forearm, finding myself in the unique position of wanting to fix a relationship, not break it.

"It's nice that Nate knows your order." I infuse my voice with an artificial perkiness. "My mom claims that boys aren't attentive to the needs of others."

Viola doesn't speak, doesn't look at me. The silent treatment continues. I grin at Nate. His eyes glint, an unspoken dare I can't resist.

"My mom doesn't know this from firsthand experience." I lean back in my chair. "She only had one child. Me. But as we lived on a commune she had exposure to boys." I talk and talk and talk. Nate adds very little to the conversation. Viola says even less, continuing her frosty silence.

The waiter returns, places a huge steak in front of Nate and a salad that wouldn't feed a bird before his mom. Viola pokes at her food, her top lip curled in disapproval, seemingly unaware I haven't received whatever his son has high-handedly ordered for me.

"Don't worry about me," I tell them. "I'll just sit here and slowly starve to death."

The doors swing open and the delicious scents of curry, coconut, cinnamon, and garlic waft into the room. My stomach rumbles and my mouth waters.

A man in a chef's hat and a double-breasted jacket bustles toward me, a plate in his hands. "Specially made for the miss." He sets it before me with a flourish. "Wattakka Kalu Pol maluwa, a dish from my country."

"No way." My eyes widen. "You made me Sri Lankan pumpkin curry?"

"Ahhh . . ." The chef beams. "Miss knows pumpkin curry." He gestures to the plate. "Try mine, please."

I lift a forkful of the curry and white rice to my lips. The flavors explode in my mouth, exotic and authentic, combining heat and sweetness. "Mmm . . ." I close my eyes, savoring the experience. "This is Nirvana on Earth."

Nate shifts beside me, pushing his leg against mine. I open my eyes and meet his gaze, see his open need, his stormy eyes promising sexual delights. I shiver, warming all over, my taste buds tingling and my body humming.

"Whenever you come to my restaurant I will make this for you," the chef declares. "I must cook more, make more people happy." He returns to the kitchen, moving quickly.

"That looks disgusting." Nate's mom finally speaks, her perfect nose wrinkled.

"It looks disgustingly good and it tastes even better than it appears." I grin at Nate, touched that he ordered this dish for me, that he wanted to make me happy. "Here." I offer him a forkful of pumpkin curry and rice. "Try this masterpiece, lover."

Nate's eyes glimmer as he closes his straight white teeth around the tongs. My heart races and my pussy moistens. His sinful mouth is within kissing distance, tasting of spices and heat.

Nate chews slowly, holding my gaze. I skim my tongue over my bottom lip and he swallows hard. "It's good." His voice is low and deep. "But it doesn't have your secret ingredient."

"No, it doesn't." Does he know the secret ingredient is love? I drift my fingers over the back of his hand, caressing his knuckles. "I'll attempt to duplicate this entrée in the future using my secret ingredient."

"I'd like that." His lips lift into his small smile and I glow.

We eat. Nate cuts his steak into precise strips, listening as I chatter about the different curries I've tried, many nationalities having been represented at the commune. Viola says nothing, picking at her food, acting as though she is seated alone at the table, her indifference driving me bonkers.

"You must have some stories to tell about Nate, Viola." I try to include her in our conversation. "What was he like as a child?" I glance at the man by my side. "Was Nate naughty?" His lips curve around his fork.

Viola's gaze flicks to me. She wants to say something. I see the need in her frosty blue eyes. She merely requires a push.

Pushing is my specialty. "He must have gotten into some trouble. Come on, Viola. Share."

"Why?" His mom sets down her utensils. "Why do you care what he was like as a child? Nathan's not going to marry you. He's like his father that way." Her voice crackles with bitterness. "And don't try the pregnancy trick. That doesn't work with the Lawford men either. Naïve girl that I was, I thought I'd be set." She shakes her head, not one hair on her beautiful head moving, the tendrils frozen in place. "I didn't know he'd refuse to marry me or that he'd be so tight with his funds."

I reach for Nate's hand and grip his fingers. His mom is telling this to me, a stranger. How many times has he heard the mercenary reason he was conceived?

"He's a real-estate developer. You'd think he'd buy me a house," Viola continues her tirade. "But, no, I'm living in a penthouse in Pacific Palisades. He—"

"Viola." I interrupt her, having heard enough. "You won't ever mention the pregnancy trick again, understand?" She opens her mouth. "It makes you look like a fool."

Her eyes blaze. "If Nate had been a better son—"

"Nate is the perfect son. He's handsome, intelligent, successful, nice. Anyone who spends two minutes with him knows that." Crimson rushes up Nate's neck, my executive adorably embarrassed. "And they also know who's responsible. You raised him. On your own. That's something to be proud of."

Nate's mom turns her head and stares at the wall, twin spots of color high on her cheeks, her frail chest rising and falling.

Nate wraps one of his arms around me, pulling me closer to him. He sips his water. I devour the last forkful of pumpkin curry. A scary silence fills our alcove. Did I break their relationship even more?

"Do you have my envelope?" Viola's voice is small. She doesn't look at either of us.

Nate reaches into his jacket pocket and extracts the bulging white envelope. "This is for the month." He slides the envelope to his mom.

She stands, avoiding my gaze. "I'm free on the fifteenth." Viola tucks the envelope into her purse and hurries away from the table, leaving him with no words of good-bye, no hug, no sign of affection, of love.

Nate and I watch her leave. Yep, I made their relationship worse. I sigh. "Sorry about that."

"Why are you sorry?" Nate grins, his eyes glittering with genuine joy. "My mother suggested a date. She's never done that before."

His mom has never suggested a date before. It takes me a couple of seconds to understand what that means. "She wants to see you again." I beam. "See. Your mom does love you." I bump against him. "But I lost the challenge. I don't think your mom will call me."

"Mentioning L'ongle was a good try," Nate acknowledges. "If she hadn't told you Frederick was the best, you would have won."

"Yes." I nod my head. Nate's mom is a proud woman. She'd never admit she was wrong. "I set that up incorrectly."

Nate pats my hip, silently agreeing with me. We sit in the small restaurant, watching the action around us, enjoying each other's company. The waiter clears the table and Nate distributes more folded bills, paying for the service as he pays for his mom's time, the touch he craves, and me.

I yearn to tell my careful controlled man that I love him, that I never wanted his money, that he is all I need, but one soul-shaking revelation is enough for today. "Thank you for arranging the pumpkin curry for me," I say instead.

"I thought you'd like it." Nate helps me stand, placing

one of his arms around me. His hold on me is necessary. My legs tremble.

"I loved it." I love him.

He leads me through the busy restaurant, his hand resting possessively on my hip, declaring to the world that I belong to him. Patrons and staff stare at us. I concentrate on the dynamic man beside me.

"Every man in this restaurant wants you," Nate murmurs, his lips vibrating against my earlobe. Blissful tremors roll down my neck. "They envy me, knowing I'll soon be inside you."

"They can want me." I press into Nate's body, seeking to be closer to him, needing more of his delectable scent, his heat, his strength. "They can't have me. I belong to you. Exclusively."

"You're mine." The car is waiting for us and more dollar bills exchange hands, Nate tipping the doorman and the valet.

"I'm yours." I settle into the passenger seat, the interior smelling of new car and freshly showered man.

Nate closes my door, rounds the hood of the black sedan, fills the driver's seat. He drives quickly, smoothly, silently. I open the windows and cool air flows over us, caressing my skin.

"Will you be making an appointment for this afternoon, lover?" I stroke his thigh, relishing the contrast of soft fabric stretched over hard muscle. "Because I need you . . . badly."

"I can't last until the afternoon," Nate confesses.

Chapter Nine

WE CONTROL OUR desires during the drive back to the office and the elevator ride to the finance floor. We exit the car, holding hands, sexual tension sizzling and snapping between us.

Gladys, the finance department's gatekeeper, studies us, her glasses balanced precariously on the end of her tiny nose. "Good afternoon, Mr. Lawford." Her gaze drops to our linked fingers. "Miss Trent."

Nate doesn't slow his pace, pulling me over the threshold and down the hallway. I laugh, thrilled by his eagerness. Employees stand in their cubicles gawking at us as we pass them, their mouths open and their eyes wide.

Yes, he has definitely claimed me. Office gossip is faster than the Internet. The entire building will know about our relationship by the end of the day.

Nate rushes me into his office and slams the door behind us. "Camille." He captures my lips, crashing our bodies together, flattening my breasts against his chest, curving his palms over my ass.

I submit, giving him total access, opening completely to him. He surges into my mouth and sucks hungrily on my tongue, his tug and pull setting off fires within me, moistening my pussy, tightening my nipples.

This isn't enough for Nate. He advances, forcing me to move backward until my ass collides with the desk, its unrelenting edge pushing into my softness.

"I need to be inside you now." Nate lifts me onto the hard wooden surface and spreads my legs, hiking up my skirt.

"Take what you need, lover." I shimmy out of my panties and open my blazer, freeing my breasts from the built-in bra. Cool air wafts over my skin and I tremble with excitement, anticipation. "You have me. You will always have me."

"I will always have you." Nate lowers his zipper and pushes down his pants and boxer shorts, revealing his long rigid cock. Pre-cum already glistens on his tip. "Not for one month." He positions himself between my thighs and clasps my hips, his grip firm, possessive. I wrap my legs around him, hooking my ankles over his ass. "Always." He thrusts deep, burying himself completely in my wet heat.

"Always," I confirm, clinging to his shoulders, tilting my hips to take in all of him. His base presses against my soft feminine folds and he stills, allowing me to adjust to his invasion, to the delectable fullness.

I stroke his nape, touch his handsome face, trace his defined chin. This man is mine, a part of me, today and tomorrow. He might never love me, likely won't ever marry me, but our energies will be meshed forever, permanently entwined.

Nate covers my lips with his and reaches under my jacket. His tongue explores my mouth and his fingers blaze along my spine, rough and warm and sure. I shrug the garment off my shoulders, giving him more skin to touch, to claim.

He rumbles his appreciation into my throat, his lips vibrating against mine. I gaze at him, at the thunderclouds of passion gathering in his dark eyes, and I quiver with excitement, gripping him tighter, ready, willing, and eager to ride the building storm.

Nate rocks into me, his movements shallow and slow, gentle steady drops of pleasure eroding my control, wearing away at my restraint. I meet and match his rhythm, undulating against him, splaying my fingers over his back, touching as much of his body as I can.

He rounds his spine, scattering kisses over my chin, my neck, my collarbone. I recline on the desk, drawing him above me, savoring the breadth of his shoulders, the power in his cotton-covered chest, the strength in his male form.

Nate fastens his lips over my right nipple and sucks hard, pulling a cry of surrender from my throat. My inner walls close around his shaft, increasing the delectable friction, escalating my already wanton desire.

He sucks on my breast as he pushes in and out of my pussy, synchronizing the tempo of his mouth and hips, the dual assault curling my fingers and toes. My nipples throb, my body clenches and releases, and my nerve endings dance.

I rake his back with my fingernails, searching for skin, and lightning flashes in Nate's eyes, a jagged bolt of electricity illuminating his soul, the force of his passion compounding my own. He drags his mouth across my skin and covers my left nipple, continuing his sweet abuse. I hitch my hips upward and dig my heels into his ass, encouraging him to move faster, to take me harder.

He nips my skin and I arch my back, the pain exciting me. "More," I urge, gripping his shoulders. "Make me feel you."

Nate drives into me with a heart-pounding force, slapping my ass against the desk, pushing the air from my lungs. I lift into his thrusts, matching his ferocity, his passion, his need.

"Yes," I shout with delight, flinging myself into the storm, no fear in my reckless heart. This is natural and right, our extremes and our rough edges smoothed by each other. I'm no longer fighting the universe, battling enemies only I see. I fit. I belong.

Nate has also changed, warmed beyond recognition. He grunts against my neck, his body folded over mine. There's not one sliver of ice remaining in his muscular form. He churns with molten emotion, the fury of his passion fully unleashed, beautiful and real.

A sheen of perspiration covers my curves, slicking our sensual slide. My thighs shake. My breathing grows ragged. I'm nearing release, a fulfillment I can only find with my unbending executive.

Nate skims my neck with his teeth, sending bursts of pleasure down my spine. I grip his shoulders with my fingers and his shaft with my inner walls, torturing him as he tortures me. We struggle, two strong personalities linked together, having one purpose, one goal.

"Camille," Nate rumbles. Beads of sweat form on his forehead, the droplets glistening on his golden skin. He's glorious and mine.

"Not yet." I cling to him, not ready to end this encounter, wishing we could fuck forever. When he's inside me everything is perfect. I'm perfect.

He ravishes me with his cock, mouth, hands, an all-elements assault decimating my resolve. I grit my teeth as the tremors rock my body, this storm too wild even for me to ride.

"Fuck," Nate curses. "Can't." He reaches between us, finds my clit, and rubs. I sob, my need for release nearing the point of pain. "Fuck." His breath blows on my ear.

I should give him the permission he requires, but that isn't possible. I'm past talking, past thinking, barely hanging onto my sanity.

Nate taps my clit and I scream, shattering, torn from the earth, lifting into the air. I clench down on his shaft, clutch his ass, suck his neck, trying to hold on, to secure myself to him.

Nate roars and thrusts hard, bathing me with warmth, with his cum. I slide along the desk as he pushes, seeking to be farther inside me. My fingernails dig into flesh. He drives into me once more and holds his pose, his gaze meeting mine, a feral satisfaction reflected in his eyes.

His shoulders shudder and he collapses, flattening my writhing body, forcing me to be still, to accept him, this. I wrap my arms around him, holding him tight.

"I love you." The words escape my kiss-swollen lips before I can stop them.

Nate stiffens, his muscles flexing under his jacket, and says nothing. I blink, struggling to contain my foolish disappointment. He doesn't value love, thinks it muddles relationships, and I know why he feels that way, know why he'll never change his stance.

This doesn't soothe the pain in my heart. I look up at the white ceiling tiles, the man destined to emotionally destroy me cradled between my thighs. I've changed too much to go back.

Unable to fight my fate, I press my lips against Nate's golden skin and wait for his breathing to level, the heaving of his chest to ease. It doesn't. The tension within him remains, painfully palpable.

I've ruined everything with my rash declaration of love. "Nate?" I thread my fingers through his short hair, the strands soft.

"I violated our agreement." He pushes away from me and fastens his pants. "I said I wouldn't come until you gave me permission." He doesn't meet my gaze. "You didn't give me permission."

Nate and his agreements. I tell him I love him; he worries about a clause in our contract. "Don't sweat it."

"Don't sweat it?" He glares at me, his eyes blazing.

"You deserve the best. And I'm clearly . . ." He stalks to the floor-to-ceiling windows, stares at the sky, his back turned toward me.

"You're clearly the best." I walk to him, my legs unsteady. "That's the problem, stud. You were too good." I stand beside my executive. "Your touch purged all of the words from my brain." I slip my hand into his and gaze at the sky. "I tried to give you permission and couldn't. All I could think about were your hands, your mouth, your cock."

He stubbornly looks straight ahead, his shoulders squared and his spine straight.

I sigh. "You're more than enough for me or for any other woman, Nate. I love you the way you are." His fingers close tighter around my hand.

We stand side by side, woman and man, intern and executive, rebel and rule setter, as different as two people could be yet connected. A bird soars high into the sky, its wings outstretched, gloriously free. For once in my conflicted life I'm not envious of the tiny creature. I'm exactly where I want to be.

"Did you really put when you could come in our contract?" I ask, breaking the silence.

Nate's lips lift, his small smile capturing my heart once more. "You should read the contract."

I laugh, joy bubbling inside of me. "Someday I'll read our infamous contract. I'm sure it will be an eye-opener."

I check my watch. The lunch hour is over and it's time to return to reality. "You have another meeting and I have to revolutionize the technology industry."

I gather my jacket, donning the garment, the leather hugging my generous curves. "Miss Yen believes in my project, did I tell you that?"

"Once or twice." Nate watches me, his expression cool, his emotions contained once more. "Does the funding mean that much to you?"

"The funding means nothing. I'm a hacker. I can find the money." I bend over and retrieve my black lace panties. "I need the mentoring that comes with the funding. I don't know what the hell I'm doing."

Nate's eyes gleam. "That's never stopped you before."

"That's true." I laugh. "I love you, Nathan Lawford. You calm my crazy ass down." I toss him my panties.

He catches the flimsy lace in one of his hands, snatching it out of the air. "I'll mentor your crazy ass."

"You'll mentor me?" I ask, stunned by his offer. Nate gives me a curt nod. He'll mentor me. He believes in me, in my project. "For how long? For the month?"

"For as long as you need me." He stuffs my panties in his pants pocket and strides toward his desk. "I'll put that commitment in our agreement."

"You do that." I laugh.

I RETURN TO my shredding room office and work all afternoon. There's no one and nothing to disturb me and I'm in the zone, coding like a woman possessed. I blast my music between phone calls, dance whenever I suffer from numb bum, and think about Nate too freakin' much.

He believes in me, he accepts me, he doesn't want to change me, and I love him with all of the passion in my wild heart. I'll do anything for him, even conform. Or try to. I haven't been successful at conforming in the past.

At ten minutes to four my phone rings. The display says Lawford Incorporated. This is Nate's billionaire father's holding company. "Hello," I answer semipolitely, curious why anyone there would be contacting me.

"Miss Trent." The man's voice is rougher, more rushed than Nate's, but there's no mistaking the connection. "Meet me at the corner coffee shop at four o'clock."

I wait for him to explain why. He doesn't elaborate, the man's expectation that I'll do what he says confirming his identity. "Nate has another meeting at four o'clock, Mr. Lawford."

"My meeting is with you, Miss Trent, not my son." Nate's dad clips each word.

"I—"

There's a click, followed by silence, the senior Mr. Lawford assuming I'll drop everything and rush to meet him. "The irony is he's right," I mutter to myself as I smooth my hair and reapply my lipstick. He has piqued my curiosity, the reason for the meeting enticingly mysterious.

I exit the shredding room and walk along the hallway, skimming my moist palms over my gorgeous leather suit. Mr. Lawford is a busy man. He doesn't make casual appointments. He wants something from me.

I enter the empty elevator car. My image is reflected in the mirrored walls, the lights shining on my green hair. This can't be about my . . . ummm . . . investigations. I've only hacked into Mr. Lawford's systems ten or eleven times and I was very careful, covering my trail, closing all of the doors behind me. His cybersecurity team couldn't have caught me. They aren't that skilled.

I stomp through the lobby, my heels ringing on the marble floor. Jerome, the nasty security guard, isn't at his post. The sleepy security guard reclines in the chair, his arms crossed and his head bowed.

I blast through the revolving doors and stride into the sun. This meeting has to be about Nate. I march toward the coffee shop, my tread heavy. His dad's employees moved my things. He'll know we're living together.

Our lunch with Viola could have been another catalyst. I kick a loose stone and it skitters over the sidewalk. Nate's dad is a very competitive man. He wouldn't like that Viola, a woman he views as an adversary, knows more about his son than he did.

I enter the coffee shop, the scent of java filling my nostrils. Quiet conversation buzzes. A long line of jittery patrons curls around the front counter.

Mr. Lawford wouldn't stand in line. I scan the space and quickly locate him. He sits alone in one of the three coveted booths, his head bent over a cup of coffee, his hair gray and his profile strong. His navy-blue suit is perfectly fitted to his large body. He exudes arrogance and power.

Standing to his immediate right is a massive brute in an ill-fitting black suit. His eyes are shielded by sunglasses, his feet braced apart, and his arms crossed.

Great. Nate's dad brought muscle to this meeting. I trod toward them. He's expecting hostility. "Mr. Lawford."

The bodyguard steps in front of me, blocking my access to his employer. "Mr. Lawford isn't interested."

"Then Mr. Lawford shouldn't have phoned me, chuckles." I rest my hands on my hips and tilt my head back to gaze up at the overly serious man. "I'm a busy woman. I have things to do."

Chapter Ten

I STARE AT the bodyguard. He doesn't move, doesn't say anything. Three middle-aged women wearing white pants and matching pastel sweaters watch us, whispering behind their hands. I shift my gaze to them. The gossiping gals scatter, squawking with distress.

"Miss Trent, I presume." Ice drips from Mr. Lawford's lips. He's definitely Nate's father, frosty to the bone.

The bodyguard moves.

Mr. Lawford gazes at me. I lift my chin and gaze back at him. His eyes are the same color as Nate's, the palest coolest gray, and his face is hard, weathered by life.

Seconds pass as we size each other up. He's a fellow game player, an older, more cynical male version of myself, a tough man known in the business world for his unwavering opinions and his unyielding stances. Has he made up his mind about me?

"You're not who I expected," he concedes.

I release the breath I didn't know I was holding. "I'm not who anyone expects."

"Have a seat." Mr. Lawford waves one of his hands. He doesn't bother to stand, sending a clear message: I'll have to earn his respect. "We have matters to discuss."

"I can't imagine what those matters could be." I smack down my ass on the brown pleather seat.

"Can't you?" He lifts his eyebrows. "Your official job title might be intern, but I know who you are, Miss Trent." He begins his verbal assault, taking the offensive. "I know all about my son and his so-called girlfriends. I know he pays you, that you're a whore, a woman who can be bought for a few dollars."

I rear back, reeling from this surprise attack. I hadn't expected Mr. Lawford to be familiar with Nate's sexual history, to know about his son's unique preferences.

I've finally figured out why being Nate's money honey is a bad thing.

"Speechless, Miss Trent?" Mr. Lawford's eyes gleam. He believes he's subdued me.

He doesn't know I've been playing these games my entire life. "Yes, I am speechless," I admit. "I didn't realize Nate's feelings about me were so obvious."

His dad blinks twice, his reaction signaling a direct hit. Score one point for me. "You're his whore," he rumbles.

"Exactly. I'm not *a* whore. I'm *his* whore." I smile, not bothered by the name-calling. I have green hair and an even crazier outlook on life. I've been called worse things. "He's paid for sex in the past yet I doubt you contacted any of those women. You phoned me because Nate cares about me. I make him happy and that bothers you. Don't you want your son to be happy?"

"Temporary happiness has a long-term price." Mr. Lawford's jaw juts out. He loves Nate. He's attempting to protect him, to stop him from making the same mistakes he did.

"I'm not Viola." I touch his hand. His skin is rough, creased with wrinkles. "I'm not trying to trap him."

"No, you're not Viola. You're honest about your intentions, about who you are." Mr. Lawford allows the contact for one telling moment, as hungry for touch as his son is. Then he draws his hand out of my reach and curls his palms around his cup of coffee. "You're open about wanting my son for his money."

"I'm open about being your son's whore," I correct him. "I don't care about his money." Mr. Lawford frowns. "You may know about Nate's so-called girlfriends, but you don't know about me."

"I know you have a price. All women do." He withdraws a pen and a check from his inside jacket pocket. "What is it, Miss Trent? How much will it cost me for you to leave my son alone?" His gold fountain pen is sleek and beautiful. I suspect it's the best.

"The person with the pen holds all of the power," I say quietly, and Nate's dad glances sharply at me. "I'm a hacker, Mr. Lawford, and I'm very good at what I do. If I wanted your money I'd take it, and there'd be nothing you could do to stop me."

He twists his lips. He doesn't believe me. I study the

check on the table, memorizing the account number. Proving my abilities will be embarrassingly simple.

"Name your price," Mr. Lawford states. "Will a million dollars suffice?"

"A million dollars?" I laugh loudly, and heads turn. Patrons watch us, their eyes wide with curiosity, their lips moving. "Is that the going rate for the perfect son? And you based Nate's worth on what? Your tally of his childhood expenses?"

Mr. Lawford's expression could freeze water. Score another point for me. "The only other person who knows about that spreadsheet is his mother."

"And Nate," I add. "Nate knows exactly what you believe he's worth."

Mr. Lawford flinches. "He wasn't meant to see that."

"Nate has more than simply seen it. He has a copy of the spreadsheet." I know what Mr. Lawford is feeling right now. In the past I've also hurt others, been too consumed by my games to realize the pain I was causing. I almost lost Kat, my best friend, that way.

"Two million dollars is my final offer." Mr. Lawford returns to the negotiations, using money to mask his emotions . . . as his son does.

"One day with Nate is worth more than two million dollars. One touch of his hand, one of his small smiles, one of his rare laughs is worth more than your entire net worth." I turn my head and stare at the picture of coffee plants hanging on the brown-painted wall, struggling to control my emotions. "He's a good man, Mr. Lawford. You should be proud of him. He's respected and loved."

"You can't love him," Mr. Lawford bluntly states. "Love doesn't exist."

"Your son doesn't believe love exists either." I smile sadly. "Unfortunately for my heart, I know love is very real." I stand, tired of this game, no longer wanting this victory. "Your concerns about us are unnecessary. Nate and I have a contract. Our agreement is for one month only. If you know your son you know he rarely extends contracts."

"I taught him that," Mr. Lawford claims proudly. "Requests for extensions erode power. Set the length of a contract and stick to it." He thumps the tabletop with his fist.

Nate won't extend our contract. A bone-deep weariness fills my soul. "Your son likes to be touched," I tell Mr. Lawford. "Shake his hand when you can. Hug him if you're able."

I stride out of the coffee shop, ignoring the stares of the other patrons. The sun is still shining and the sky remains blue. Tall palm trees line the sidewalk.

Only I've changed. I walk quickly, heading toward the small park, my sanctuary amid the concrete and steel madness. Returning to the office isn't an option. My emotions are too bare, too exposed.

The park is deserted. I sit on a shaded bench, remove my shoes, and sink my toes into the grass, grounding myself in nature. The tree's leaves rustle above me. A bee buzzes near the gleaming white gazebo. I breathe in, breathe out, inhaling the fragrance of the surrounding flowers.

My relationship with Nate will end and my heart will break. That is a certainty. My pride must remain intact or I won't survive it. I unclip the phone from my waistband and access the free Wi-Fi connection.

It takes me an hour to hack into one of the private banks Mr. Lawford uses, my signal relayed through multiple servers, concealing my trail. It takes me minutes to move the money, reducing four of his nine accounts to zero balances.

Mr. Lawford phones me soon after I empty his bank accounts. I see his number on the small screen and ignore him. He calls again and again and again. I focus on my data-sharing project, working remotely.

At five o'clock Nate calls me. Unable to hear his voice, my emotions still too raw, I don't answer his call. Coworkers rush from the tall concrete-and-glass office building into the steel-and-glass buses. No one enters the park, not a single person taking the time to enjoy nature, to savor the hot summer day.

The building will be devoid of life. I should return to my office. Unable to dredge up the energy to move, I stay on my park bench.

Moments pass. The sun sinks lower and lower in the sky. The murmur of voices fades. The sense of sorrow, of loss lingers.

Nate was never mine to keep. I'm a vacation for him. Mourning our relationship is foolish and I'm not a foolish woman.

The hairs on the back of my neck lift, my body hums with awareness, and my mood lightens. I know who has arrived yet I don't look at him, fearing what he'll see in my eyes. The wooden bench slates dip and a warm firm thigh presses against mine.

"Are you angry with me?" Nate places one of his arms around my shoulders.

"If I was angry with you you'd know it." I stare at my dirty feet.

Nate chuckles softly. "That's true." The silence stretches. He pulls me closer to him, the contact soothing me. "Someone hacked into some of my father's bank accounts."

I dig my toes deeper into the grass, seeking rich dark earth.

"He thinks I know something about it." Nate pauses. "Should I know something about it?" I don't say anything. "The hacker had access to other bank accounts, accounts with larger balances, and she didn't touch those funds. Accumulating wealth wasn't her goal."

"Accumulating wealth has never been my goal." I rest one of my palms on Nate's right thigh. His muscles flex under the fabric.

"Why did you choose my father?"

"Ask him why." I've already interfered too much in their relationship. "Tell him I'm okay with telling you everything. I own every word I said."

"You always do." Nate twines a strand of my green hair around his index finger. "My father can be . . . challenging at times."

I glance at Nate, see the concern reflected in his eyes. "He loves you."

"I don't know about that." Nate tugs on my hair.

"I do." I touch his gorgeous face, unable to resist him. He turns his head slightly, pressing his cheek into my palm, his skin warm and smooth. "Your dad doesn't know how to show it, but he does love you."

Nate smiles sadly. "Showing emotion isn't a Lawford strength."

"I have that strength in spades." I slide my fingers over his nape, pull him toward me, cover his lips with mine, putting everything I feel into the kiss, all of the love and all of the passion.

Nate groans into my mouth and our tongues twist, tumble, his mint flavor causing my cheeks to tingle. He threads his fingers through my hair, cups my skull, holding me to him as he dives deeper inside me.

Nate doesn't love me, his mom hates me, and his dad thinks I'm a whore. Our future is doomed, our contract nonnegotiable, and my heart will be broken. This moment makes all of this agony worthwhile.

Nate sucks on my tongue and my fingers and toes curl, the pressure divine. I caress his cheeks, his jaw, his neck.

My stomach growls. Loudly. My face heats.

Nate laughs. "I suspected you'd be hungry." He stands, pulls me upright. I slip my dirty feet into my shoes. "I had groceries delivered to our house."

Our house. That sounds so nice, so right. I allow him to lead me back to the office building, our hands fused together, our fingers entwined.

"I'll help you with dinner, the key word being help." Nate's tone is light and happy, edged with a boyish excitement. "I've never prepared a meal for anyone, not even for myself."

"Never?" I stare at him. "But cooking is such a joy."

Crimson creeps up Nate's neck. "Joy isn't a Lawford strength either."

I SHOW MY sexy executive the joy of cooking, teaching him how to chop, stir, taste, and laugh. We dance as the curry simmers, Nate twirling me around the center island. He closes his eyes while I add my secret ingredient. I kiss the air above the spoon and then kiss him. We set the kitchen table together, the dining room too formal for our needs. I chatter while we eat, and Nate listens, all of his attention focused on me.

His phone rings while I'm packing our lunches for tomorrow. Mr. Lawford has been calling all evening.

Nate places plates in the dishwasher. "Has my father suffered enough?"

I glance at my watch. "He has three more minutes of suffering left." I programmed the funds to automatically transfer, restoring Mr. Lawford's accounts to their full balances.

Nate's lips twitch. "I'm sure he'll never do it again." He draws me to him. "I'll talk to him tomorrow. Tonight is ours."

I lean into Nate's hard muscle, his enticing warmth. "Tonight *is* ours." I gaze at him, memorizing every inch of his face, knowing our time is limited. "I love you, Nate." I brush my fingertips over his square chin. "Never doubt that." I trace his lips. "Ever." I smile. "Do you have to work?"

"Yes." Nate playfully nips at my fingertips and I snatch my hand away. "And you do too." He lifts me to the counter. "But first I want dessert." He pushes my skirt upward and spreads my legs, his hands rough and arousing.

"We didn't prepare anything for dessert." I tremble in anticipation. I'm bare, completely exposed to him.

"Didn't we?" Nate bends over, fastens his lips to my left knee, and sucks. I squirm, swishing my ass against the enameled lava countertop. "You taste ready." He switches knees and marks more of my pale skin, his suction exactly right. "And you smell." He breathes deeply. "Delectable." His breath gusts against my inner thighs and I quiver.

He strokes up and down my legs, his fingers roaming close to my wetness but not touching, never touching, and I heat to simmering. I unbutton my jacket and drop it to the tiled floor. The cool air puckers my nipples.

"Let me look at you." Nate opens me more to him. "You're smooth and white." He peruses me closely, his golden head positioned between my legs, his gray glacier gaze fixed on my pussy lips. "Pink and wet, succulent with desire." He extends his tongue and licks one thigh and then the other, leaving trails of sizzling sensation on my skin.

I groan and cup my breasts, ruthlessly squeezing my curves. My hair cascades over my shoulders, the strands as straight and as soft as a bolt of green silk.

My temperature continues to climb as Nate plays with

my body, and I writhe over the countertop, seeking coolness. He watches me, his predatory gaze staking a claim
on my heart and my soul, his hands dancing over my
moving form.

"Touch me, love," I demand, pinching my nipples, the
pain escalating my desire. "Fill me with your fingers."

Nate's eyes sparkle with humor. "Dessert should be
savored." He fans my folds and I shiver, the contact sending waves of heady bliss over my body, drawing more
moisture from my core.

"Screw savoring dessert." I follow his fingers with my
hips. "Gobble me up."

Nate chuckles and rubs his thumbs over my clit. I
swallow my curse. He's a dreadful man, my sexy executive, torturing me with an almost gleeful enthusiasm,
reveling in my frustration.

He kisses along my legs, over my mons, his love pecks
increasingly intense. "Yes," I murmur encouragement.
"That's what I need." Nate flicks his tongue over my folds,
diving into my crevices, exploring every intimate inch of
me, and I grasp his blond head, holding him to me.

Nate skims my entrance, circling round and round.
I move my hips, mirroring his actions, my ass brushing the countertop's hard surface. He pushes his tongue
inside me, rasping his flesh against my inner walls, and
I cry out, twisting my fingers in his short hair, seeking a
handhold.

My world is deliberately chaotic, every norm, every
rule challenged. Nate is my anchor, my steadfast man,
and I hold onto him, lifting my hips as he fucks me

with his tongue, devouring my pussy, brushing his nose against my clit.

Nate growls, the animalistic sound unexpected and thrilling. He throws my legs over his shoulders and cups my ass, his grip secure and tight. I buck against him as he eats me with a mind-blowing gusto, thrusting his tongue inside me again and again.

"Love," I pant, my chest tight, my arms and legs shaking. "Love," I repeat, unable to find more words, my brain filled with one thought. I love him. I love this incredible man. He licks, nibbles, pulls on my pussy folds, demolishing the remnants of my restraint, teetering me over the edge of release.

"Love?" My voice stretches with need.

Nate fastens his lips over my clit and looks upward, meeting my gaze, his eyes as dark as night. I read his intention, my breath catches, and he sucks. Hard. I scream, bucking upward, smacking my pussy against his face, ecstasy flowing over me.

Nate flings an arm over me, holding me down, as he pulls on my sensitive flesh, his tanned cheeks speckled with moisture. I twist and wiggle and writhe, struggling to be free, my satisfaction too intense, colors exploding in my brain.

Nate's grasp on my body is unbreakable, his suction transcendental. The waves of bliss gradually lessen and I still, my limbs heavy and my heart light.

Nate gently lowers my legs. "You're right." He straightens, licking his lips, his hair spiked by my fingers, his face flushed and wet. "You're delicious." His eyes glow.

"Am I?" I gaze at him, dazed.

He gathers me in his arms. "The sweetest I've ever tasted."

"And you've tasted many women." I wrap my arms around his neck, too high on his touch to be jealous. Other women might have held him in the past, but he's my man now.

"I've only tasted one woman." Nate presses his lips against my forehead. "But I know she's the best." He holds me tight.

I smile sleepily. His escorts took their no-kissing rule very seriously. "Your sex life must have really sucked."

"My entire life sucked." He nuzzles his chin into my hair. "And I didn't realize it until I met you."

"Hmmm . . ." I close my eyes, savoring his words, his heat, his scent.

Chapter Eleven

WE WORK INTO the early morning hours, our computers set up in Nate's home office, our chairs positioned side by side, each of us focused on our own projects while spending time together. I'm in harmony with him and at peace with the world.

When our minds no longer can function Nate leads me to my new room and we make passionate love, calming our bodies. I fall into a deep dreamless sleep, my cheek pressed against his tanned chest. He'll leave me during the night, I suspect, maintaining his part of our arrangement, an arrangement I no longer want.

My predictable man isn't as predictable as I think. I wake up in his arms with his chest gently rising and falling against me and his breath blowing on my hair. The sun's rays stretch across the bed, lighting his golden skin, warming me.

Nate smiles in his sleep, his face relaxed and his blond

hair mussed. "You're so handsome," I whisper, tracing his straight nose with one of my fingertips.

"Is that why you agreed to our arrangement?" He opens his eyes, his irises the palest coolest gray. "Because, as my father learned yesterday, you didn't need my money."

"You wouldn't have allowed me to touch you if I hadn't taken your money." I circle his flat male nipple with the tip of my tongue, tasting the salt of his skin. Nate's body hardens, his muscles flexing tight, his cock growing rigid against my left thigh. "You needed that." I flick his skin.

He rolls me onto my back and stares down at me, studying my face, his expression serious. "And what did you need?"

I lift my knees, cradling him between my thighs. "I need you." He eases inside me, stretching me open, filling me. "Not your money or your gorgeous face." I dig my short blunt nails into his shoulders, the slow slide fraying my nonexistent control. "I need you, love."

Nate stills, his cock buried inside me. "You would say that." He rests his forehead against mine, his breath blowing hot against my lips, his chest flattening my breasts, his weight heavy and arousing. "You're perfect."

"I'm only perfect when I'm with you." I run my palms over his back, savoring his strength, his overwhelming maleness. "When I'm with you I fit." I tilt my hips and he pushes deeper.

"You fit me too well," Nate groans. He covers my lips with his, kissing me thoroughly, leisurely, with a heartbreaking tenderness, a caring I didn't think possible.

His hip rock and I move with him, matching him stroke for stroke, the connection between us tight and secure, almost unbreakable.

We make love slowly as though neither of us wishes for this encounter to end. I caress him all over, investigating the breadth of his shoulders, the slope of his spine, the small of his back. He's my peace, my love, my freedom, all of my beliefs rolled into one sexy man, and I give him the touch he needs, learning the curve of his firm ass, his muscles clenching and releasing as he fucks me.

Nate pushes in and out of my mouth and my pussy, his tongue and cock sharing the same rhythm. My lips hum and my heart pounds, desire building, building, building. I wrap my legs around him, coaxing him to move faster, faster.

He complies, breaking our lip-lock and gliding his cheek along mine. Nate advances and retreats, advances and retreats, pushing me toward the point of no thought and no return. The headboard bangs against the wall, the noise punctuating his thrusts, and a sheen of perspiration covers his skin, these proofs of exertion exciting me.

"Yes, love, harder." I rise up, meeting each drive forward, smacking our bodies together, warmth radiating from the points of contact. This is where I belong, my chaos contained by Nate's unrelenting form, his cock surging in and out of me, his grunts echoing in my ear.

He remains too controlled for my liking. I rake my fingernails over his back and he arches his spine, pushing into my punishment, embracing the pain.

"You're wild," I exclaim, exhilarated by my Iceman's heated reaction.

"I'm wild for you." Nate nips my bottom lip, the sweet agony cascading down my neck, over my chest, connecting with my pussy. I shake, rippling beneath him. He sucks my marked flesh as he thrusts into me again and again.

"I'm close," I admit, passion coiling around me, stealing my breath. "When I come," I pant, "you come." I grip his shoulders, staring up at him.

"We come as one." Nate meets my gaze. His eyes are dark and shine with emotion. Rivulets of moisture drip down his cheeks, glistening on his skin.

"One," he bellows as he drives into me with a toe-curling force. I hold on, Nate swivels his hips, grinding against my clit, and the tight band of desire stretching across my chest snaps.

I scream, levitating off the bed, the sheets tangling around my legs. Nate slams me back down on the soft mattress, restraining me, taming my anarchy. I fight him as I fight everyone. He doesn't free me, and in my heart I know this is right, this is how it is supposed to be, how I am supposed to be.

He pushes deeper inside me as he fills my body with his hot cum. My pussy constricts and relaxes, constricts and relaxes, milking every last drop from his cock.

"Fuck." Nate collapses, flattening me. I murmur a protest and he rolls, taking me with him, our bodies and souls connected. I ride the rise and fall of his chest, feel the quieting of his inner storm.

A warm blanket of comforting silence falls upon us. I breathe deeply, savoring his scent and his touch, my heart filled with love. He cares for me. I know this in my soul. He might even love me, though the words are trapped inside his chest.

"We agreed to sleep in separate beds." Nate drifts his fingertips over my ivy tattoo, tracing each leaf, each curve in the vine. "I violated our agreement."

I look at him. The lines etched between his eyebrows reveal the breadth of my rule-setting man's concerns. "Thank you." I cuddle closer to him. "You broke the rules to make me happy and that means a lot to me."

Nate's frown deepens. "I didn't break the rules to make you happy," my rigidly honest executive confesses. "I broke the rules to make *me* happy."

He wants to sleep by my side, to spend time with me. Isn't that love? "That means even more to me." I smile at him. "I love you, Nate."

Nate's lips part and I hold my breath, certain he'll finally say the words back to me, finally tell me he loves me. He bends and presses those parted lips to my forehead, once more saying nothing, giving no indication of how he feels.

Struggling to contain my disappointment, I exhale slowly. "You truly suck at pillow talk." I roll away from him and stride toward the bathroom, leaving the most gorgeous man I've ever met lying naked in my bed.

WE GET READY for work. I shower and don the next suit hanging in the closet, a matte black leather suit with double slits in the skirt and a corset-styled jacket, laces cinching the waist.

We make breakfast together, Nate mastering the toaster while I fry the eggs. I tease him about setting off the smoke detectors. He gives me that small smile of his. I ask his advice about an issue I'm having with a subcontractor. He suggests some options. I don't tell him I love him again. I know what his response will be.

By the time we reach the car I'm all talked out. We drive in silence, with the windows open, the morning air cooling the vehicle. My backpack rests by my feet. I'm carrying Nate's lunch as well as my own.

I watch the activity around me. A dark-suited man in a red sports car talks on his phone while changing lanes. A harried mom in a minivan drives with only one hand on the wheel as she tries to control a bawling boy in the backseat. Nate's face creases with more and more lines, his fingers tightening on the steering wheel, his body rigid.

"You're worrying about something," I observe. "Spit it out, love." I place my hand on his upper thigh. "You'll feel better."

Nate's lips move, making no sound. I force myself to wait and wait and wait, patience not a strength of mine.

"I'm not good at pillow talk," he finally blurts

"No shit, Sherlock." I roll my eyes. "Tell me something I don't already know."

"I have no idea what you expect," Nate explains. "Pillow talk isn't covered in our agreement." I grit my teeth, tired of hearing about our damn agreement. His gaze shifts to my face and then back to the road. "I don't want to disappoint you. It's better if I say nothing." His knuckles whiten.

"No, it's not better if you say nothing." I cover his hand with mine. "If you ever disappoint me I'll tell you and you'll fix it. I'm not the type of person to stay quiet about . . . well . . . anything."

Nate says nothing, the lines on his face remaining.

"We'll likely have a monster fight. I'll give you the finger and curse you out and you'll get all icy and sexy." I shiver, heating up simply thinking about our imaginary skirmish. "This will enrage me even more and I'll slap your chest, setting off the sparks between us. You know how it is when we touch." I move my hand to his upper thigh and he hardens, his cock pressing against the fabric of his black dress pants. "Then we'll have wild crazy make-up sex, putting a few dents in that immaculate desk of yours."

I pause. He doesn't say anything.

"What do you think?" I ask.

"I think wild crazy make-up sex sounds good." Nate's lips lift into his small smile, the creases between his eyebrows flattening.

"That's all you got from that tirade, huh?" I laugh and skim my hand over his fabric-covered cock.

He turns the car into Blaine Technologies' underground parking lot. "I have an eight o'clock meeting."

"And I must cause turmoil in the mobile world." I regretfully move my hand back to his thigh. "Wild crazy make-up sex will have to wait."

Nate parks the car and covers my hand with his. "I don't know what I'd do without you, Camille."

I suck in my breath. This is as close to a declaration of love as he has ever come. "And you said you're not good at pillow talk." I bounce out of the vehicle, my spirits light, and sling the straps of my backpack over one of my shoulders, not feeling its weight.

The limousine is parked in the corner. The same three black sedans and silver Jaguar are slotted in their regular spaces. I'm arriving with the same man and he wears the same black suit, white shirt, and black tie he always does.

For once this repetition, this normalcy, doesn't make me squirrely, doesn't make me want to snarl and snap and fight the establishment. Nate takes my hand, leading me to the bank of elevators, and I follow him, blissfully content.

"You know we *will* fight, right?" I press my body against his. "Ours will never be a peaceful relationship. I have a bit of a temper."

The elevator doors open. "I've noticed." Nate enters, turns, draws me to him, his hands resting on my leather-clad ass. "You get angry, we fight, and then we have make-up sex." He shrugs. "I can live with that."

I tilt back my head, gazing up at him, my green hair cascading down my back, loose and free. He is smiling, his eyes sparkling, his face devastatingly handsome and unguarded, not a trace of his renowned coolness in his countenance.

"I can live with that too," I murmur, my voice husky, my body aroused. I want him. I always want him.

The doors open at the ground floor. Nate stiffens and I move to his side.

Jerome, the security guard, my nemesis, enters, his gray uniform pulled tight over his protruding stomach. He presses the button for the fourth floor.

"Mr. Lawford." He nods to Nate. "Miss Trent." Jerome scans my body, his gaze lingering on my breasts and legs.

Nate places a possessive hand on my hip.

"All interns must enter and exit through the front doors." Jerome doesn't heed Nate's unspoken warning, the security guard's full attention fixed on my breasts. "I'll be reporting this violation to Mr. Henley."

"Miss Trent is with me." Nate's voice chills to unadulterated arctic frost, his words dripping with a glacier arrogance. A shiver of excitement rolls up my spine. He's powerful and mine. "I enter wherever I like." My Iceman is back and he's very pissed off.

Jerome gulps, his Adam's apple bobbing, his eyes widening. "M—M—Miss Trent now reports to you, sir?"

"I consider Miss Trent to be an extension of me." Nate pulls me closer to him. "Treat her as you would any top executive."

"Yes, sir." Sweat trickles down Jerome's face, his lips quivering. The big bully looks as though he's one sharp word away from peeing his pants.

I can't suppress my smirk. Take that, rent-a-cop. Nate squeezes my hip, his chin tilted upward, his profile strong and proud. We stand side by side in silence, watching the red digital numbers ascend.

The doors open at the fourth floor and Jerome rushes out, moving faster than I've ever seen him move. A sweat stain marks the back of his uniform.

"Did he search you?" Nate asks as the doors close once more, his words scarily soft.

I blink at him. "What?"

"Did he search you?" my angry executive repeats. "Because if he has touched you I'll make him wish he had never heard of Blaine Technologies."

Whoa. I stare at Nate, incredibly turned on by this surprising display of jealousy. "No, he never touched me." I lean against my protective man. "He searched my bag and stuck his finger in my lunch, but he never searched my person."

"Good." Nate's chest heaves, his eyes blazing, his rage not completely spent. The doors open. "This is your floor."

"And you have an eight o'clock meeting." I balance on my tiptoes, brush my lips against his. "Try not to kill anyone today." I laugh as I exit the elevator.

Nate loves me, though he likely doesn't know that yet. We have a month together. That's enough time for him to accept his feelings, to say the words, to make a longer commitment, to take a chance on forever.

The low-talking brunette approaches me, smiling shyly, her gaze darting to my face and then away. I wish her a boisterous good-morning and she beams, her face lighting up, her lips moving, her words too quiet for me to hear.

Nate loves me. My chest bubbles with happiness. My project will gain the mentors it needs. The sun has risen and it is a glorious day.

Everyone receives a greeting from me this morning, even the pinch-faced lady. She mutters about noisy people and printer fumes as she sprays the air with a product I can only describe as poison in a can.

"Green," Miss Yen hollers.

"Good morning, boss." I flounce into her office, a big smile plastered on my face. Miss Yen is seated behind her desk, which is unusual for my hyperactive boss. She's wearing yet another beautiful black suit, her hair twisted into a tight chignon.

"You're my favorite boss, did you know that?" I chirp, ecstatic with the world.

Miss Yen winces. "Sit down, Green." She doesn't meet my gaze.

My fantastic mood fades as I obey her. Someone is in deep trouble, and I suspect that someone is me.

Chapter Twelve

MISS YEN FIDGETS in her seat, appearing as uncomfortable as I feel. I must be getting fired. I've bent the rules one too many times and she has to let me go.

I set my backpack on the carpet. This isn't a first firing for me. I know what happens next. "Should I pack the rest of my things?"

Miss Yen jerks back her head and meets my gaze. "What? No." There's another long stretch of silence and she sighs. "A project came back from the dead and the Change the World grant no longer has an opening. You won't be pitching at the end of the month."

I won't be pitching. I hired the subcontractors, worked late last night, hoped for nothing. The disappointment threatens to crush me, a huge weight sitting on my chest, pressing down, down, down.

I breathe in, breathe out, breathe in, breathe out, forcing air through my lungs, struggling to contain my feelings. This fiasco isn't Miss Yen's fault and she shouldn't have to deal with the emotional aftermath. She believed in me.

"Our agreement about you using the shredding room still stands," my boss says, her voice soft. "There will be an opportunity to pitch next year, but you're resourceful, Green. You won't wait for that opportunity. You'll find another way to fund it."

"I *will* find another way to fund my project," I assure her. Funding is the simple part. I need the mentoring, the collective brain of Blaine Technologies' impressive management team. They're too busy to help a lowly intern.

Miss Yen watches me closely, as though she worries I'll go ballistic. It's a legitimate concern. The data-sharing project means everything to me and I don't have the knowledge to manage it alone.

I'm not completely alone. I curl my fingers into fists, digging my fingernails into my palms, using the pain to offset my disappointment. Nate promised to mentor me and he always keeps his word.

"Thank you, Miss Yen." I grab my backpack and drag my rejected ass to the shredding room, shutting the door behind me. My makeshift office isn't where I want to be.

I want to take the elevator to the seventh floor, rush past Gladys' desk, down the hallway, into Nate's office. He'll strap his big strong arms around my body, pull me onto his lap, and hold me tight as I cry.

That isn't an option. Nate has a meeting until nine o'clock. And I won't cry here, alone, with the cameras pointed at me, capturing every tear, every weakness.

Slumping into my seat, I stare into space and twirl the green fountain pen in my fingers, clinging to this flimsy connection to Nate. I have to do something, anything, or I won't be able to hold it together.

Working on my beleaguered project doesn't appeal to me. The thought of talking to subcontractors, acting as though everything is okay, as though the project isn't on life support, is painful, taking more than I have to give. Shredding files doesn't require brains or feigning happiness. I stomp out of my temporary office into the hallway, the force of my exit smacking the door against the doorstop. The thud is obscenely loud and the pinch-faced lady complains. I turn my head toward her, not hiding any of my grief, and she shuts her mouth.

I grab a box of files and heft them back to the room. The sanctioned destruction calms me. I feed the papers into the shredder and the machine chews them into thin strips. The result is predictable, controllable, giving me a sense of accomplishment, of confidence. Rational thought returns.

I have Nate. He promised to help me. The two of us will figure out a solution to this mess. We'll save the project and make a difference in the world.

At nine o'clock I wipe the white dust off my hands, smooth down my skirt, and exit the room semiserenely, like a normal human being would.

I take the elevator to the finance floor. The trip is quick and the car is thankfully empty. As I exit Gladys, the gatekeeper, looks up from a stack of papers. "Mr. Lawford is in his office, Miss Trent." She sounds relieved to see me.

I frown. "I don't have an appointment." Why is she expecting me?

"He needs you." Gladys' phone rings. She glances at the number but doesn't answer it. "He's not himself." Her voice drops to a whisper.

"Okay," I reply. He's not himself. I don't know what that means, only that it's bad.

I hustle along the hallway. Employees stand in their cubicles, their faces turned in the same direction, their heads tilted as though they're listening to something of great importance.

Having blown out my eardrums at too many clubs, my hearing isn't the best. I only hear the employees' hushed tones, the wave of whispers cresting as I pass. My heels thump against the carpet and my heart pounds. What's happening?

I turn the corner and Nate's voice reaches me. "You called her *what*?" he bellows. The employees around me collectively gasp. I doubt they've ever heard their Iceman boss bellow, ever seen this passionate side of him. I *am* familiar with this side of Nate and even I'm stunned, the depth of his emotion both thrilling and frightening me.

"You think you know, but you don't," Nate grumbles. "You don't know about her. You don't know about us. You don't know me." His office door is wide open, his one-sided conversation traveling throughout the quiet office. He'd be mortified if he knew this. I increase my pace, determined to protect his icy reputation, to protect him.

"I don't care what she said. That's not who she is. If

you call her that again or interfere in our relationship in any way, I will sever all ties with you."

I cross the threshold and close the door behind me. Nate stands before the floor-to-ceiling windows, his back to me. He holds the phone in his right hand, his knuckles whitening around the device. His left hand clenches and unclenches a ball of black lace.

He's clasping my panties, I realize.

"No, I don't want your money," Nate says, his voice edged with disgust. "Opening your wallet won't fix this situation. It isn't that easy."

I wrap my arms around his waist and press my chest against his rigid spine, brushing my cheek over his soft suit. He leans back, pushing into my touch.

"You can't put a price on trust, Father." Nate shakes his head. "Money debases its value," he says, echoing my words.

He drops the phone to the carpet, and I hold him to me, stroking his suit-clad chest with my fingertips, attempting to ease his turmoil, to calm my angry man.

"Your dad loves you," I murmur. "Everything he did, he did out of love."

Nate slides my panties into the pocket of his pants and he turns. "My father called you a whore, Camille." He gazes down at me, lightning flashing in his storm-filled eyes. "No one calls you a whore."

"You're paying me for sex." I place my palms on his chest, savoring his solid body, his strength. "I *am* your whore."

Nate pulls me closer to him, folding my curves into his muscle. "You didn't deny his accusation."

"I couldn't deny it." I tilt back my head and study my handsome executive. "It's the truth." This confrontation won't be the last one. Anyone who knows Nate's history with women will assume I'm an escort. I won't ever be able to refute it.

"It's not the entire truth." He brushes my hair away from my forehead and presses his lips against my forehead. "You accepted the money for me."

"I signed the agreement for you," I admit. "I'd do anything for you. I love you."

Nate cradles my face between his rough hands and covers his lips with mine. I grasp his shoulders, meeting him kiss for kiss, molding my tongue to his. He tastes of mint and man, of sweet propriety and heady decadence, and our connection rights the imbalance within me, restoring my strength and refilling my emotional reserves.

Nate draws back, breaking our embrace. He studies my face. "I'd do anything for you also." He stalks to his desk, pulls out a familiar stack of papers, and returns to my side. "I want you to shred this." He hands me our contract, his expression serious.

"This is our agreement." A hard lump forms in my throat. "We need this."

Nate's lips twist. "You haven't even read it."

"*You* need this," I revise.

His gaze drops to the papers in my hands and returns to my face. "This contract isn't what I need."

Nate doesn't need the contract because he doesn't need me. He's dumping my rebellious ass. "No." I step backward, pain piercing my heart, my soul. "I won't allow you to renege on our deal." My voice breaks. "Not today, not on the same day I find out I won't be pitching my project to the executive team, find out I did all of that work for nothing, hoped and dreamed for nothing."

Nate flinches. He didn't know the pitch session was canceled. I read that truth in his eyes. "Camille—"

"We have an agreement." I wave the papers in the air, not allowing him to speak, fearing his words. "And I'm not releasing you from it. So suck it up, buttercup. You're stuck with me. I—"

"It's over, Camille," Nate declares, his subzero tone decimating my protests. "I'm fixing this." His gaze holds mine, his gray eyes pale and cold. "I'm fixing everything."

My heart splits into two. "Shredding our contract won't fix anything."

"Yes, it will." He clasps my icy hands, his skin surprisingly warm. "What we have now isn't a normal relationship. You know this has to end."

I do know this, but I can't accept it. "We're not normal. We'll never have normal relationships. And we have a month left in our contract." I lift my chin, blinking back my tears. He can fall in love with me in a month. "This doesn't have to end today."

"It ends today," my unrelenting man replies, his voice firm.

"I can change," I plead, past pride, past everything.

Nate squeezes my fingers. "I don't want you to change."

He doesn't want me. Period. I pull my hands away from his, unable to bear the contact. "We have an agreement." I try again. A tear trickles down my cheek and I brush it away. He's made me cry, the bastard. "You can't simply terminate an agreement whenever you want."

"If you'd read the contract you'd know I *can* simply terminate our agreement." Nate smiles and I want to scream. My heart is breaking and he's happy. "There's a cost. I must pay you for the entire month."

I stare at him. "You must pay me?" I hear the hysteria in my voice. He thinks I care about the money. Has he learned nothing about me?

Nate nods. "I'll transfer the funds into your bank account this afternoon."

"You're transferring funds." My entire world has imploded and he's calmly settling his account, putting the final line in his Camille Joplin Trent relationship spreadsheet. "After all of the time we've spent together, the things we've talked about, the love I've showed you, you're offering me money?" I shake with fury, my rage matching my agony.

His lips part.

"Fuck you, Nate." I tuck the cursed contract under my right arm and flip him the double bird, extending both of my middle fingers. "You can keep your precious cash." I fling the door open. "That isn't what I want from you. That was never what I wanted from you."

I stomp along the hallway. Employees duck their heads, hiding in their cubicles. The floor is eerily quiet, the heaviness of my tread accentuated. I feel Nate's gaze on my back. I don't turn around.

I pass through the reception area and Gladys' mouth drops open. She doesn't say anything as I jab the button sixteen times, taking my rage out on the little illuminated circle.

The elevator doors open. A dark-suited man smiles at me. I glare back at him and he gulps, hastily exiting the car. The button for the second level of the parking garage has been pressed.

Not fit for human company, I punch the button for the ground floor. Nate spurns his father's monetary offer and then he says he'll pay me? I replay every sentence of our conversation in my mind. He makes no damn sense.

The elevator doors open and I rush through the lobby. My heels bend against the marble floor. A cautious woman would tread more lightly. I slam my feet down with all of my strength, the noise waking the sleeping security guard. He jerks in his chair, grabs his holster, sees it's me, and closes his eyes once more.

He doesn't think I'm a threat. He doesn't realize how dangerous my mood is. I blast through the revolving doors, step outside, and glower at the sky.

The weather should be dark and stormy, reflecting my pain. It isn't. The sky is blue, the clouds white and fluffy, the sun shining. I curse LA's perfect climate as I head toward the tiny park, my shoes battling the hard sidewalk.

I turn onto the gravel pathway and gravity claims its victory. The heel of my right shoe snaps, rendering it completely useless. I color the air with another long stream of profanities, yank both of my shoes off my feet, and toss them into the garbage can. Good riddance to bad shoes.

Tiny stones bite into my bare soles. I hobble onto the grass and locate the nearest bench. A connection with the earth usually grounds me. Today I need more. I need Nate.

Cursed man. I slap the contract and my ass down on the wooden slates. Leaning back, I stretch my arms along the back of the bench. The sun's rays caress my face and the wind rustles the leaves. Nothing feels right.

Nate thinks shredding the contract will end what we have. It won't. My body, heart, and soul are bound to him today, tomorrow, forever. Destroying a stack of papers won't change that.

I thumb through the pages, skimming the words. Nate will pay me a small fortune every day I'm with him. He'll replace my entire wardrobe, every item detailed including the number and brand of socks he'll buy. He'll provide three meals a day, three snacks, and more beverages than a healthy woman should ever drink. I'll have a bedroom with a walk-in closet and an attached bathroom. I'll receive a minimum of two kisses and one orgasm a day. Everything he will give me is absolute, specific, and almost lovingly outlined.

Nothing he receives is certain. I dictate what I do, say, eat, and wear. I decide whether or not we have sex. I can decide to give him no orgasms, not to kiss him back, not to touch him. He doesn't curtail my freedom at all.

Because Nate didn't craft our agreement to control me. I hold the papers against my chest. He was ensuring he didn't disappoint me, guaranteeing my expectations would be met, trying to make me happy, to take care of me.

And I hadn't even taken the time to read it.

My phone buzzes. I glance at the screen. I've received a meeting request for next Tuesday at five o'clock with Mr. Blaine, the CEO and founder of Blaine Technologies. The subject is mentoring and the meeting reoccurs once a month for a year.

I accept, of course. I may be rash and reckless and completely heartbroken, but I'm not an idiot. Having Mr. Blaine as a mentor is the equivalent of winning the lottery for any entrepreneur.

I'm his wife's friend. That must be why I've landed these highly coveted meetings. He heard I was working on a project and wishes to help.

A small voice inside me whispers *bullshit*. This voice, originating from the region around my heart, knows Anna hasn't arranged these mentoring sessions.

Three minutes later I receive another invite. This monthly after-hours meeting is with the chief marketing officer, a man whom I've only met once in my life. I accept, stunned by my sudden popularity, and the voice inside me grows louder.

Anna, my friend, has baby brain. She wouldn't have arranged this second meeting. She doesn't care enough.

Only one person on the planet cares this much. He knows what this project means to me and he promised to fix everything. He always keeps his word.

As I accept one meeting I receive a request for another. By ten o'clock I have monthly meetings set with almost all of the executive team. I also have no doubt about who is driving this activity.

Nate calls me, his number appearing on my phone's

small screen. I shouldn't answer. My emotions are exposed, my soul vulnerable. But I can't not speak to him, can't forgo this opportunity to hear his voice, maybe for the last time.

"Camille speaking," I answer, striving for a professional tone while my heart pounds in my chest.

"This is Nate," he says. There's a long gut-twisting pause. "I never listen to hip-hop. I don't know any of the songs."

He called me to talk about music? I shake my head, confused. "I'll send you my playlist."

"I'd like that." There's another long stretch of silence. Papers rustle and a chair creaks. "A couple should know each other's favorite songs."

A couple? My hands tremble. "I thought you ended our relationship."

"I ended our agreement, not us, never us," Nate clarifies. "I want us to have a normal relationship."

He never ended us. My heart squeezes. He wants to spend time with me, be my lover. "Nate, love, we'll never have a normal relationship." I smile, dazed by his revelation. "I grew up on a hippie commune. I'm a hacker, a former Goth girl. I have green hair and a tattoo and multiple piercings. I don't know what normal is."

Nate chuckles, the sound low and deep. "I don't know what normal is either. And I don't want normal. I want you. I want you to choose to be with me."

"I always chose to be with you." I cradle the phone against my face, wishing I could touch him. "I consulted my heart, not the contract, when I made decisions."

The line goes quiet. Nate wants a normal relationship.

We could start with a normal conversation. "If you don't listen to hip-hop what do you listen to?" My bet is on classical. Nate seems like a Beethoven type of guy.

"I listen to country." He surprises me.

"Country?" I laugh, unable to picture my sophisticated executive wearing a cowboy hat and boots. "Why?"

"I like the lyrics," Nate explains. "The singers talk about real life, real emotions." We yap about music, TV shows, movies, neither of us having much time to indulge in either of the latter. The topics are intentionally light, steering away from more serious issues. I tease him about his eclectic tastes, his not caring about popular opinion. He likes what he likes, screw the critics, and I love that about him. I love him.

We finally end the call. I glance at my phone's screen and blink. An hour has passed. I gingerly navigate the hard gravel, the stones digging into my bare feet. Nate cares for me. The hot sidewalk sears the tiny wounds on my soles. He might not love me, but I know he cares for me.

I enter the office building. The cool air blasts my heated cheeks. The equally chilly floor tiles soothe my aching feet.

"Walk with me." Mr. Henley, the big brutish head of cybersecurity, appears out of the shadows and matches my stride, his scarred face hard, his suit, shirt, and shoes as black as night. He doesn't walk casually with anyone. He's stalking me for a reason and that reason isn't good.

I'm in trouble. Again. "Mr. Henley." I suspect not wearing shoes violates Blaine Technologies' rigid dress code. We enter the elevator. I press the button for the legal floor. Mr. Henley presses the button for his floor.

"Due to security concerns I don't normally mentor anyone outside of my department," Mr. Henley rumbles.

I nod, knowing this information. When I first joined the company I had brazenly asked him to mentor me, and did some extremely stupid things to try to impress him, almost losing Kat's friendship in the process. Mr. Henley had turned me down cold, threatening to fire my defiant ass.

"But as your mentorship request comes from Mr. Lawford, I'll make an exception," the scary executive concedes. "I owe him a few favors and this is the first time he has collected on one."

Mr. Henley owes my strong and silent man favors. I gulp. Nate constantly surprises me, keeping me challenged, excited, head-over-heels in love with him. "Do many of the executives owe Nate favors?"

"Yes." Mr. Henley's dark eyes gleam. "We all owe Mr. Lawford favors. He's a good man, Camille, and he cares for you. Try not to break too many of his rules."

"Many of his rules need to be broken," I mutter, Mr. Henley's insights secretly thrilling me. "Do you truly think he cares for me?" I ask.

"A couple of months ago an urgent business issue arose. I tried to talk to Mr. Lawford about it in the parking garage." Mr. Henley shifts his weight from one foot to the other. "He said he'd meet with me at eight o'clock, told me he had an elevator to catch."

"I was taking that elevator car," I share. "Nate wanted

to see me." He has cared about me for months, before we touched, before we kissed.

"I'm aware of that," Mr. Henley says dryly. "I suggest you find your shoes." The elevator doors open. "And remember that the cameras in the elevators and the shredding room are fully functional." He steps out of the car.

Nate and I had sexual encounters in both places. I grin. We must have given Mr. Henley's security team quite a show.

Chapter Thirteen

As I ENTER my shredding room office, the soothing scent of mint fills my nostrils, a fragrance I will forever associate with Nate. The lush green herb is set on my desk. Its shiny white pot matches my executive's black-and-white kitchen.

A folded piece of fine white card stock leans against the plant. Nate's distinctive handwriting flows in heavy black ink across its surface.

> *I humbly request the honor of your presence for lunch.*
> *Twelve noon.*
> *My office.*
> *No RSVP is necessary.*
> *Nate*

I trace the words and smile. This wonderful man is courting me, quirky crazy Camille Joplin Trent. He's making one of my secret dreams come true.

I access Nate's schedule, prepared to set up the appointment for lunch. This isn't required. He has already blocked the hour, today, tomorrow. My heart skips a beat. Forever. Ten years from today's date there's a meeting labeled Lunch With Camille on Nate's busy timetable.

The default for executive meetings is private, with only the participants having access to the details. Nate has designated our lunch dates to be public. Everyone in the company will see he's spending this hour with me.

Forever.

He loves me. And I love him. I know what he needs, what will make him happy. I spend the next thirty minutes painstakingly changing our contract by hand, tweaking every clause using the green pen Nate gave me. My Iceman needs this agreement, needs this structure, as I need the freedom to rebel, to express my emotions, to be me. I embrace and love this part of him.

Mr. Henley sends me a recurring meeting request. I'll accept it later, my focus now on my relationship with Nate. I can't change the world without him. We're a team.

I clip the pen to the first couple of pages of the amended contract, hug the document to my chest, and exit my makeshift office, humming as I move along the hallway. A strange calmness falls upon me, a sense of rightness.

I should be freaking out. With this new agreement I'm committing to Nate forever, establishing rules I'll be forced to follow, setting expectations I'll have to fulfill. The crazy thing is I *want* to follow these rules. I *want* to fulfill Nate's expectations of me. I *want* forever.

I press the button for the elevator once and the doors open, the elevator gods rewarding me for my restraint. The car is empty and the trip is express, the only stop being the finance floor. I don't have time for second thoughts.

Not that I have second thoughts. I'm more certain about this, about us, than I've ever been about anything.

I exit the elevator car. Gladys is seated at her post. She glances down at my bare feet and sighs. "Mr. Lawford is expecting you, Miss Trent." She places her palms on her desk and pushes her plump body out of her chair. "I'll bring you to him."

I raise my eyebrows. "That isn't necessary. I know the way."

"That *is* necessary." Gladys walks along the hallway and I follow her, matching her slower pace. "Mr. Lawford has designated you as a tier-one guest. Tier-one guests are escorted to his office. They have unlimited access to him. If you need to speak to him and he's in a meeting, you can call me and I'll locate him."

I'm designated as a tier-one guest. This is how important I am to Nate. "Whoa."

"Yes, whoa." Gladys smiles. "Mr. Blaine, our CEO, is the only other guest Mr. Lawford has designated as being tier one."

I'm on par with his boss. Nate loves me. I know he does.

The floor is quiet. I catch glimpses of faces, Nate's employees furtively watching us as we walk toward his office. Gossip spreads like wildfire in an office. I stand straighter. Everyone will know how much Nate cares for me.

We approach his office. The door is closed. "I'm canceling Mr. Lawford's meetings for the day." Gladys pushes her glasses up on her nose. "He's a good boss, Miss Trent. His team would do anything for him, and we want him to be happy."

"That's what I want too, Gladys." I summon a smile, determined to meet this new challenge.

"I know." The receptionist raps her knuckles on the door. "Mr.—"

Nate swings the door open, his presence sucking all of the oxygen out of the space, leaving me breathless. "Thank you, Gladys," he rumbles. "That will be all." He doesn't look at his receptionist, his gaze fixed on my face.

His black suit, white shirt, and black tie are immaculate, his collar and cuffs stiff and perfect. His golden hair is darkened with moisture, as though he has recently showered. There's no shadow of stubble on his defined jaw. I inhale. He smells delicious, fresh and sexy and overwhelmingly male.

Nate is studying me closely, his expression hungry, warm, no trace of the Iceman in his handsome face. "You came."

"I haven't come yet." I speak softly, conscious of the ears listening to our conversation, wishing for only him to hear me. "But I'm hoping you'll rectify this problem."

Nate's lips lift, his pale gray eyes glimmering with unspoken promises. "I'll add it to our list." He guides me into his office and closes the door behind me.

A table for two has been set up in front of the windows. "Is this the best seat in the house?" I tease. The tablecloth and china plates are pure white, the silverware shines, the crystal wineglasses sparkle, and the electric candlesticks flicker.

"Our meals will arrive soon." Nate takes my left hand, lifts it to his lips. "I thought we'd talk first." He turns my hand and presses a kiss into the center of my palm. My fingers tremble. "Get to know each other more."

He's opening all of his doors to me. "*Or* we could negotiate first." My voice is husky. "And then have wild crazy make-up sex." I press my body against his, giving him the contact I know he craves.

Nate hardens, his eyes darkening. "Camille." He slides his hands down my back, leaving a trail of decadent sensation.

"We should talk first." I tear myself away from his sexy physique. He needs the structure of our agreement as much as he needs my touch. "I amended our contract." I wave the papers.

"I asked you to shred that damn thing." My sexy executive scowls. "You're not my whore; you never were, and I won't tolerate anyone insulting you, hurting you."

"Good." I saunter to the guest chair, swaying my hips. "Because I hurt myself enough as it is." I lift my right foot, showing him my sole.

"What did you do?" He rushes toward me. "You're bleeding." He drops to his knees, carefully encircles my ankle with his fingers and examines my foot. "Sit," he commands, his voice allowing no refusal.

I sit down, bemused. He strides to the small bar fridge near his desk, extracts a bottle of water, and returns to my side. "There's a reason our dress code requires shoes," he grumbles, wetting his handkerchief. "I'll ask Gladys to buy you some flip-flops. Until then you aren't walking anywhere."

"How will I get around?" I smile, his overreaction confirming my suspicions. He loves me. He must. "Will you carry me wherever I want to go?"

"Yes, I'll carry you." Nate carefully dabs the soft white cotton over my skin, his blond head bent, his gaze focused on his task, on me. "And I'll take care of you."

"Because you love me." I say the words he won't.

"I don't know if I love you." Nate turns his attention to my left foot, his touch gentle and caring. "Because I don't know what love is," my brutally honest executive confesses. "I've never felt like this before. When you're hurt I want to kill whoever caused you pain. When you're sad I want to hold you. When you're disappointed I want to fix the problem."

"Like you fixed my project issues, lining up the mentors for me." I pet his perfect hair, the strands short and silky. "What else do you feel?" I push him for more, needing to be certain, to have no lingering doubts.

Nate gazes up at me, his eyes gleaming. "All you have to do is look at me and I feel powerful and alive, as though there's nothing I can't do. My world is warmer, brighter, filled with joy and laughter. I belong as I've never belonged before."

"You fit." My voice cracks. He nods. "That's love, Nate." I smooth his eyebrows. "That's how I feel about you."

He neatly folds his handkerchief, the white square now black with dirt, and places the fabric on a corner of his desk. "Expressing love isn't a Lawford strength." Nate's lips flatten. "I don't know how to be the man you deserve." He cups my bare knees, his palms rough and warm. "I don't know how to earn the right to someday be your husband."

He wants to marry me. I struggle to control my emotions. "That's why we need an agreement." I hand him the contract. "It's merely a place to start. If a clause doesn't work for us we'll amend the agreement, try something different."

Nate stands and leans back against the desk. He fans the paper once, twice, three times, the pages fluttering. Silence stretches and anxiety builds within me.

"You eliminated the per diem payment," he finally says. "Good. We don't need that clause. I'll always take care of you, Camille."

I can take care of myself. I open my mouth to protest.

"Because I want to take care of you," Nate adds. "Forever." His gaze meets mine. "I require forever, Camille. You're the type of woman a man, once he loves, will never be able to release."

He wants forever. This is how much he loves me. "Those are my terms also." Emotion chokes my words.

"Then we have a deal." Nate turns to the desk, unclips my pen, flips to the last page, and signs our agreement, scrawling his name across the white linen paper.

"You should read the contract first, know what you're signing," I advise.

"I trust you." Nate faces me, leaving the contract on the desk. "And I love you. I'll read it later, learn how to care for you properly." The desire in his eyes curls my bare toes.

"I'm sorry I gave you the finger." My chest tightens with love, with need.

"You have no reason to be sorry. You warned me if I ever disappointed you, you'd give me the finger and curse me out." Nate's lips lift. "And you did exactly what you promised. You were so angry, so passionate, so unbelievably sexy. I was hard as a rock all morning."

I drop my gaze. His erection strains against the fabric of his dress pants, the visible proof of his passion drying my mouth. "That must have been uncomfortable during your meetings." I lick my parched lips.

"Gladys canceled my meetings." Nate discards his suit jacket, stripping slowly and sensuously, his predatory gaze fixed on my face. "She said I wasn't acting like myself." He drops his tie on the carpet.

"Was that the truth?" I unfasten my jacket and peel the leather away from my skin, freeing my breasts.

"No. For the first time in my life I *was* acting like myself." Nate flicks the top button of his dress shirt, deepening the exposed V at his throat, his skin golden against the crisp white cotton. "But she was right to cancel my meetings. I don't want anyone else to see me like this. You're the only person I trust with my soul."

"You can trust me." I lower my feet to the carpet and I wince, pain shooting up my legs.

"Try to stand and I'll paddle your ass," he warns.

I give him my most seductive smile. "I might like that, big boy."

"You won't like it, love." Nate lifts me easily onto the desk. "I'll be too angry for make-up sex." He unzips my skirt. "Too angry to put more dents in my desk." He pulls on the garment, sliding the soft leather over my legs. "Too angry to fill your tight little pussy." He skims his fingers over the jewel in my belly button.

"Too angry to love me." I shimmy out of my panties, the desk cool against my bare ass.

"I'll never be that angry." Nate yanks on his shirt. Fabric rips and buttons pop, the plastic disks bouncing on the carpet. "I'll always love you." The shredded cotton floats to the floor. "Sit on our agreement, Camille." His muscles ripple, not an ounce of excess padding on his fit form. "I want it to smell of you."

I slide the fine linen paper beneath me. "You *are* a kinky bastard, aren't you?" I wiggle, grinding my scent into the document.

"So I've been told." Nate unzips, discarding his pants and boxer shorts with one hard yank. His cock is hard, his thigh muscles defined. He's beautiful, male, and mine. My nipples tighten to the point of agony, aching for his touch. "Spread your legs for me. Show me how wet you are."

"You're being very bossy today." I narrow my eyes as I comply, opening my body to his gaze. "I'm not one of your vanilla-sex yes-women, Nate." I run my hands over my breasts, my stomach, my hips, teasing both of us. "You can't control me."

"I've noticed that." He watches me, his eyes dark with desire. "You're my green-haired hippie, believing in peace and love and freedom." My naked executive wraps his fingers around his slightly curved cock. A bead of pre-cum forms on his tip. "You're fearless, strong, defiant." He lowers his gaze to my feet and scowls. "Even when you're hurt."

"You're clever, solid, steadfast, and I need you." I gaze at him with all of the lust in my heart, telling him with my eyes what I want to do to him, how I want to lick every inch of his skin, suck on his flat nipples, take him deep inside me, find release in his arms.

He groans. "Look at me that way again and I'll come."

"You'll come when I give you permission to come, Nate." A sexy sense of power fills me. I spread my thighs wider, giving him a clear view of my cleanly shaven mons, my pink pussy lips, my empty entrance. "And you won't come one moment sooner." I strum my fingertips over my wetness, the flames of my desire burning, scorching me inside and out. "Touch yourself. Prepare yourself for my pussy."

"I'm always prepared for your snug little pussy." Nate tightens his grip on his shaft. "And I see you're ready for me." He strokes his cock, pumping up and down, up and down, his tempo matching mine. "You glisten with sweetness and smell delicious." His nostrils flare. "Ripe and womanly."

"Your pillow talk is improving, love." I circle my clit, winding my arousal around my body. We touch and tease our bodies, watching, wanting, waiting, prolonging this moment, wishing it would last forever. I drop my head back, my hair cascading over my shoulders, the tendrils caressing my skin.

"You're beautiful." Nate's eyes flash, bolts of light illuminating storm clouds. "And you're mine." He moves between my legs, stroking my calves, knees, thighs, setting off tremors of delight. "To love forever." His cock head brushes my clit and I quiver.

"Fill me, Nate." I undulate on top of the desk, calling to him with my body.

Nate cups my ass, holding me in place, and positions himself at my entrance. "I'll give you everything you want," he vows as he pushes inside me. I moan, the fullness sublime.

The invasion is slow and steady, his conquest thorough and endless, his cock filling me. I grasp his arms, savoring his strength, his muscles flexed and tight.

Nate gazes down at my face as he mounts me, raw, stark lust gleaming in his eyes. There's no need for words, his emotions and thoughts easily read, all of his doors open to me, his secrets shared.

The slide of cock into pussy finally concludes and I wrap my legs around his waist, hooking my feet above his ass, our bodies joined, our souls linked. Nate curves his palms over my breasts and strokes my nipples with his fingertips, the pleasure delectable and right. We fit, two extremes converging into a more powerful whole.

"This is everything I want," I murmur, rocking against him as he kneads my curves, his skin rough and arousing. Nate allows me to control the motion, tugging, pinching my nipples, the sweet pain driving my fervor toward the ceiling, the connection between us humming.

I writhe, grinding against him, my solid wall of a man. Nate doesn't move, standing with his back straight and his hips still, presenting an exciting challenge I can't resist. I reach above me, grip the edge of the desk, and pull, our agreement serving as a glider under my ass.

I slide until only his tip remains inside me, my body agonizingly empty, and gaze up at him. Nate lifts one of his eyebrows, his eyes glittering, daring me to fuck him.

I will fuck him. Using my legs, I slam myself against him, smacking my pussy lips against his base. He grunts, his cock bobbing inside of me, his clasp on my breasts intensifying.

"Your body is mine, Iceman." I laugh, joy meshing with my desire. I repeat the motion again and again, my arm and leg muscles straining, my pussy heating to my flash point.

"You're fearless." Nate twists my sensitive nipples and I cry out, clenching his shaft with my inner muscles. "So fuckin' fearless," he groans, his deep voice adding to my turmoil, compounding my need.

My arms tire and my desire builds. Beads of sweat form on Nate's forehead, and his body shakes as he struggles to remain still. I'm tormenting both of us with my stubbornness.

"Fuck me, Nate." I release the desk and reach for him.

"Yes." He draws me upward, flattening my breasts

against his chest. My hair ripples over my shoulders. As Nate moves against me, his rhythm slow and steady, he threads his fingers through the tendrils, then drifts his fingertips over the tattoo winding down my back, silently accepting all of me: my green hair, tattoo, piercings, and rebellious nature.

"So unique." Nate thrusts harder and harder. "Special." I hitch my hips upward, my fingers flattening against his broad back. "Mine," he rumbles. We work together, struggling for our fulfillment. My breasts smack against his chest and my ass whacks the desk's hard surface. I squeeze and release his shaft with my pussy, massaging him into a frenzy.

That isn't enough; our movements are too shallow.

"Nate?" He'll know what to do, how to please me.

"I need more." He pushes me onto my back, covers me with his big body, and drives into me.

"Yes," I cry, bouncing my heels against his ass. This is what I need, what I want. Nate pounds into me, hard and furiously fast, his skin slapping against mine, heating me to my core.

I grip his shoulders and rise into each thrust, panting, yearning, shamelessly seeking my satisfaction. We fuck on his office desk while his employees work diligently outside the door, unaware that their normally cool collected Iceman boss is balls deep in a rebel intern's hot wet pussy.

This naughtiness thrills me. I dig my fingernails into his skin, marking him as mine, and he is mine now and forever, part of my soul until death do us part. My body shakes, my orgasm approaching, as inevitable as our love, our destinies entwined.

"Two more," I gasp against his neck, my pussy coiling tight around his shaft.

"One." Nate drives into me, propelling my ass against the wooden surface, shaking my control. He withdraws and I cling to him with all of the strength in my smaller body, needing him inside of me.

"Two." He thrusts into my clenched pussy and I scream, torn apart by bliss, the room spinning around and around and around. Nate covers my lips, smothering my screams with an awe-inspiring roar. He pushes deeper, filling me with his cock and his cum, and I buck, twist, trying to free myself from his lips, his touch, the sensation too much, too exquisitely intense.

Nate restrains me as he always does, my unrelenting man providing structure and security to my anarchy, soothing my savage thoughts, gentling my rough edges. My bone-rocking tremors ease to flutters and he collapses.

"Love you," I mumble against his slick skin.

"I love you, Camille." Nate braces himself upward. His chest heaves. His eyes are dark with spent passion. I gaze up at him, unable to believe this handsome, giving, intelligent man is mine.

"Make-up sex is the best," Nate declares.

"I'm glad you liked it." I grin, splaying my fingers over his left pectoral muscle. "Because we'll have make-up sex quite often. I have a bit of a temper," I confess.

"I noticed." Nate's lips lift into that half-smile of his,

the one that drives me wild. "Your passion is one of the many things I love about you." He kisses the top of my head.

"Your pillow talk continues to improve." I snuggle deeper into his big body. "What else do you love about me?"

My Iceman chuckles.

Epilogue

"AND MR. BLAINE said they'd incorporate my app into
their new operating system," I chatter as Nate and I enter
the elevator car, holding hands. He presses the buttons
for our respective floors as he has done every workday for
the past eleven months.

I find this routine strangely comforting amid the
other changes in our lives. Emily, Mr. Blaine and Anna's
baby, is talking. Mr. Henley and Kat are married. My
data-sharing website and app have launched, Blaine
Technologies managing the project under their umbrella
of other products. I'm focusing on the ideas for the next
release stage and that suits me just fine. Making rules and
managing others aren't my strengths.

Nate is my strength. "This should expand the donation base substantially." I gaze at our reflections in the
mirrored walls. My emerald earrings, four in each ear,
sparkle. The matching hardware for my tongue, nose,

and bottom lip are just as subtle, Nate's impeccable taste pleasing Blaine Technologies' stodgy fashion police. I'm wearing a formfitting black leather suit and the sexiest shoes I've ever owned, the six-inch heels sinfully narrow. My green hair falls around my shoulders, loose and free. "What do you think about that?" I ask.

"It's a good idea," Nate murmurs. He's clad in his usual black suit, white shirt, black tie, his expression frosty and his chin raised, his cheekbones chiseled as though carved out of ice. "It'll be more exposure for the app." Thin lines form between his blond eyebrows, the telling fissures in his frigid profile triggering my concern.

"You're worried about something." I squeeze his hand. "Spit it out, love. You'll feel better."

Silence stretches. I wait, giving him the time he needs. While I may blurt out every thought passing through my brain, Nate is more careful, his caution offsetting my recklessness.

His lips flatten. "This scenario isn't in our agreement. You might get angry." His pale gray eyes gleam. "Again."

"And then we'll have make-up sex." I brush my body against his. "Again." I smile seductively. "Should I cancel my morning meetings?"

"Gladys has already canceled your meetings." Nate strides forward, waves his passcard over the elevator sensor, and slaps the emergency stop button. The car jerks and then stills, the red digital numbers stuck between two and three. "Camille." He turns to me, drops to one knee, and takes my hands, his fingers trembling.

"Nate," I squeak. He's proposing. My head spins. He wants to make our forever status official.

"I realize that marriage is an artificial construct designed by the establishment to regulate our natural desires," Nate says grimly.

"Sweet Mother Earth." My lips twitch. "Tell me you didn't ask my dad for permission to marry me." My mom and dad view the legislation of love as archaic and oppressive.

"I tried." Crimson creeps up Nate's neck. "Your dad wishes us joy and realizes we have to walk our own paths, but he refuses to serve as the authority figure in our relationship." My overly serious executive sighs. "My father thinks marriage is a trap. My mother doesn't believe Lawford men are capable of commitment. There's nothing in our agreement about marriage." The lines on his face deepen. "I don't know if this is what you want, if you'll say yes."

"Yes," I tell him, seeking to ease his concerns.

"Pardon?" Nate gazes up at me.

"Yes." I kneel beside him, the floor tiles cool and hard against my bare knees. "I'll marry you." His lips part. "No one expects us to marry, to have a traditional wedding ceremony." I hold both of his hands. "But we've never done anything people expect." I kiss his knuckles. "I'm yours forever, Nate, and I want the world to know it. I want our children to know where they belong, where they fit."

"Our children will know they were conceived in love, planned for, and wanted." Nate pulls me into his arms and presses my face against his chest. His clean fresh-showered scent engulfs me. "They'll always feel worthy." He pets my hair, his touch gentle and soothing. "Cared for."

"Loved." I loop my arms around his neck and cover his lips with mine. We kiss, touch, tease, Nate's mint flavor tingling in my mouth. He plays with my tongue stud, rotating the emerald and flicking the back, the sensation deliciously decadent. I wiggle closer to him.

Nate stands, drawing me upward with him, his taller physique supporting me, our lips fused together, one. He has been a source of strength, knowledge, and sanity during my charitable venture start-up, sustaining me through the emotional ups and downs, the long nights and endless meetings, the triumphs and the crushing setbacks. He's my rock, always there, always calm, cool, collected.

"I love you." I smile, drunk on his caresses.

"I love you too." Nate reaches inside his jacket pocket, removes a heart-shaped emerald ring, and slides it onto my finger. The ring fits perfectly, made for me, as he is, my sexy executive.

"You're my rebel heart." He lifts my hand, kisses the stone, and I melt against him, my knees liquefied by my Iceman's soul-felt words. He's hard, his cock pressing against his pants, pressing against me.

"My heart belongs to you." I shift, rubbing over him, taunting him with my body, my hands flattened against his lapels, my emerald ring glittering. "Forever."

"Forever." Nate cups my leather-clad rear, squeezing my curves, his sure grip escalating my arousal. "I need you, Camille." His eyes gleam with hunger. "I need you now."

I need him as desperately. "Then take me." I pivot on my heels and hike up my skirt, the air cool on my heated skin. "Give me everything you have, big boy." Gripping the metal hand railing, I bend over, pushing my bare ass against him. I gaze at the mirrored wall and don't recognize myself. My face is flushed, my lips pink and parted, my hair falling forward, sleek and green and perfect, the emeralds catching the light.

I'm no longer a Goth girl, fighting all of the unfairness in the world, isolated and alone. I'm now an otherworldly seductress, a sophisticated and unique young woman secure in her own power, belonging with the stunning man behind me.

"You're beautiful." Nate unzips his pants, the loud rasp declaring his intention. I wiggle, waiting impatiently for the sublime fullness only he can give me. "So beautiful." Fabric swishes, his pants and boxer shorts pooling around his ankles.

Warm rough fingers stroke along my ass cheeks and fold over my hips. I watch him in the mirror. His blond head is bent, his focus on my body, his eyes stormy, needy, laden with fierce emotion. Flesh prods my entrance, broad and unrelenting.

I spread my legs wider and roll my hips enticingly, daring him to subdue me, to claim me. Nate meets my sexual challenge, pushing inside me, skimming his cock head along my inner walls, stretching me open. As my serious man slowly works his way into my tight pussy, he meets my gaze in the reflection.

Silver sparks flash in his dark eyes, his desire melding with mine. The connection between us, always constant, always there, sizzles and snaps. A current of energy flows around our partially clothed bodies, plucking at my nipples and heating the pit of my stomach.

Nate takes me completely, pressing his base against my feminine folds, and he stills, kneading my hips with his fingertips, his chest rising and falling. "You're perfect."

"I'm perfect for you." I arch. My body is contained by restrictive leather and barricaded by mirrored wall and hard man yet I feel free, freer than I've ever been.

"We're perfect together." Nate leisurely withdraws. "This is everything." Only his tip remains inside me. "This is the best." He drives deep.

"The best," I cry, gripping the metal railing. As he pistons in and out of me my hair sways, a veil of green silk hanging downward, rippling with every thrust.

Our rhythm gradually builds, our bodies moving together, male and female, muscles and curves, tanned and pale. Nate hooks one of his arms around me and covers my mons with his palm, pressing the heel of his hand against my clit, the contact spiraling my desire upward.

He is driving me toward madness while he remains frustratingly composed, his tempo steady, carefully regimented. This is unacceptable. I undulate against him, coaxing him closer to the edge, calling him to join me so we can reach fulfillment together.

Nate answers, surging forward. I propel myself backward. Our bodies smack together. I moan with delight, my thighs quivering, my curves warming with the contact. He grunts. I pant. Skin slaps against skin, the sounds of our fucking savage and primitive.

Nate, my only safeguard against total chaos, has lost his renowned control. He plunges into my body with a toe-curling passion, taking me again and again. His chest rests on my back, his hands cover mine, pressing the engagement ring against my finger, the metal branding me.

I gaze at us in the mirror, watch as lightning flashes in Nate's eyes. Beads of sweat glisten on his forehead. The overhead lights cast a warm glow on his golden hair. He's delectable and mine and neither of us will last much longer, his breathing growing ragged and my pussy tightening around his shaft.

"When I come you come," I instruct, my voice husky.

He murmurs a reply, the words too softly spoken to decipher, and finds my clit with his fingertips, rubbing, rubbing, rubbing. I stiffen more with each graze of his rough skin, tension stretching over my shoulders, across my hips.

Nate captures my sensitive nub between two of his fingers and my eyes widen. He wouldn't, would he? He drives his hips forward, taking me hard and deep, and closes his fingers around my clit.

"Nate," I scream, bucking, writhing, this trace of pain sending me soaring over the edge, flying free. The emeralds in my ears and bottom lip bounce myriad spots of light around the small space, the stones acting as a dozen tiny disco balls, dazzling me. He pushes into me deeper and roars my name, hot cum pulsing from his cock, our connection steadying my flight.

My head spins, my body flushing hot and then cold, my limbs weakening. Nate holds me, not allowing me to loosen my grip on the handrail or fall to the floor. He keeps me safe, protecting me from my reckless self.

"I love you, my beautiful future wife." Nate straightens, drawing me against him, nuzzling his chin into the curve of my shoulder. "My forever love."

I lean back, savoring his unbending strength. His breath fans against my skin, the softest of caresses. "I love you, my handsome husband-to-be." I wiggle my fingers, making the emerald in my engagement ring catch the light. "My today and tomorrow." A peacefulness fills my soul, a sense of belonging.

Nate mouths along my neck, his lips leaving a trail of sweet awareness on my skin. "We should change the contract."

Nate and his contracts. "We have all morning to negotiate the terms." I love my impossibly rigid man. I love him with every bit of my being.

He turns me to face him. His pale gray eyes glint. "We have our entire lives to negotiate the terms." He cups my cheeks with his rough hands and covers my lips with his.

An Excerpt from

FLASHES OF ME

No one in this coffee shop knows who I am. I stand in the line, waiting to place my order. They don't know about my past. They don't know my last name. I tap my lavender heels against the floor, drumming an up-tempo tune into the tan-colored tile. They won't remind me why I shouldn't be happy.

I need to be happy. I need to laugh, to have fun, to focus on this fresh start. If I don't, I'll cry, and I promised my father I wouldn't cry. I plaster a silly smile across my face and I tap my heels harder against the floor. These two actions lighten my mood, allowing me to cope with my emotions.

The bleary-eyed woman swaying in front of me yawns, adding vocals to my beat. For LA locals, it's six in the morning. For a recently displaced New York native such as myself, it feels like nine o'clock. I'm eager to start my new job and my new life on the West Coast.

I'm two hours early. The internship orientation session at Blaine Technologies is scheduled for eight o'clock sharp, not one minute before and not one minute after. Although caffeine is the last thing I need, standing in line at this coffee shop gives me something to do and someone to watch.

I slide my gaze to the fascinating someone waiting at the front counter. The biggest man I've ever seen in my entire life looms over the cash register, his feet braced apart as though he's preparing for battle. His ebony hair is cropped close to his head, hiding nothing, and he's dressed completely in black like a villain from a 1970s spy movie.

I survey my behemoth's broad shoulders. It's all him under his jacket, not a hint of padding disturbing the cut. His suit is bespoke, custom made especially for his big body, and I suspect the designer was English. My mystery man is wearing Barker Blacks, his leather shoes as large as the rest of him. Even his matching dress shirt is well made, the collar and cuffs stiff and crisp.

He glances over his right shoulder, meets my gaze, and I inhale sharply. His eyes are as dark as his ensemble, his nose flattened and his chin square. Everything about him screams power, strength, vitality, and the woman in me responds, my nipples tightening, my breasts pressing against the blazer of my favorite lavender suit.

My behemoth returns his gaze to the frazzled barista and I exhale, my head spinning. It has been years since I've allowed myself to notice a man, to think about what

I want, what I need. My fingers tremble as I smooth my flared skirt. I want this stranger desperately, more than I've ever wanted anyone in my life.

This is a problem, as I have no idea how to snag his attention. My last date took place when I was seventeen, and I suspect flashing my breasts at a pep rally won't land me this sophisticated man. I chew on the inside of my cheek, having no other clever ideas.

I ponder my next steps, and my stranger moves away from the front counter, clasping a cup of coffee with his thick fingers. He ordered plain black coffee, no cream, no sugar, no whipped cream, and hell no to the chocolate sprinkles. My father likes his coffee the same way.

My mystery man stops at the lid and stir stick island and a stout man wearing mismatched jacket and pants rushes to the counter, barking his order at the disheveled barista. The rest of us shuffle forward in line. The tall skinny brunette behind me pleads into her sparkly pink phone, begging her boyfriend to give her one more chance. She'll be the girl he needs, she promises. She'll lose those last five pounds.

I don't know where she'll lose those five pounds. She's already as thin as a yard of fine silk ribbon. I look down at my more ample bosom, my breasts wrapped snugly in the blazer.

"No, please." The brunette sobs. "Derek! Derek!" She glances at her phone's small screen and her face crumples. My heart aches for her. She doesn't know how to hide her sorrow, not like I do. I can help her with this.

I touch the girl's bare arm, diverting her attention

away from her phone. "Who did your pedicure?" I feign an interest in her perfect pink toes. Although her beige sandals *are* adorably strappy, my goal is to distract her from her grief. "I have to know," I insist.

The brunette wipes away her tears with the back of her hand. "I—I—I—"

I glance around us fervently as though I'm afraid someone will overhear us. The behemoth is watching me, his dark eyes glinting with intelligence. Some people think big men are dumb. Some people also think blond women are stupid and no one should wear pink at a funeral. I learned long ago to ignore some people.

"Look at what happened to me on the flight here." I slip my right foot out of my lavender pumps and wiggle my big toe. A huge chip of coral polish has flaked off, revealing raw nail. "I rushed for a flight, banged into a baggage cart, and that was it. My pedicure was ruined."

The brunette's red-rimmed eyes widen. "That's terrible."

"It's a disaster." I ignore the behemoth's shaking shoulders. He doesn't understand. My mystery man has the strength to deal with loss directly. He doesn't need to pretend, to use trivial distractions as a means to cope. He would never travel across an entire country seeking to escape his sadness.

"I'm in a strange city," I explain. "I have so many cute sandals and I can't wear them." I shove my foot back into my shoe, hiding the offending toe.

As we exchange information and bad salon stories, the behemoth leaves. I watch his broad shoulders disappear into the LA sunshine and feel as though I've lost a piece of my soul, a part of my future.

I'm being ridiculous. He's a stranger. We didn't exchange a single word. I move forward in line. There's one more customer to serve and then I'll be next. I smile at the barista. She smiles back and turns this smile toward her patron. The tired lady's lips curl upward. Smiling is contagious and I've missed watching this happy virus spread. I've missed it so very much.

The lady leaves, a cup of coffee cradled between her hands, and I approach the counter. "Good morning," I sing, my spirit buoyed with joy. "I'd like a small coffee, two creams, three sugars, extra whipped cream, and hell yes to the chocolate sprinkles."

The barista laughs, the bubbly sound floating in the mocha-scented air. "The big guy is one of our regulars." She flies around the station, her apron flapping and her ponytail bobbing, her energy matching mine. "His order is always the same."

He's one of their regulars. I'll see him again tomorrow. "Thank you." I pay for my order, adding extra singles to the barista's tip jar for providing me with this valuable information.

My behemoth and I have a date . . . of sorts. My smile widens as I leave the coffee shop, my cup clasped in my hands, my tote slung over one of my shoulders. Should I buy him a coffee? I meander along the sidewalk, the sun's rays warming my shoulders. Would that be too cheesy? Tall palm trees line the path, the grass green and lush, the traffic bumper to bumper, vehicles creeping forward.

I could linger at the stir stick station, drop my lid on the floor, casually brush against him as I retrieve it. His body would be solid and warm.

I pass the glass-and-concrete-cube building housing my new employer. Blaine Technologies is in the midst of buying Volkov Industries, my family's company. The negotiations between the former rivals have been drawn out and hostile. This hostility shouldn't affect me, as I applied for the internship using my mother's maiden name, a lie my uncle convinced me was for the best.

It's still too early to arrive for orientation and I haven't yet solved my hunky man problem. I wander into a small park I discovered earlier this morning. Gravel crunches under my shoes. Thick hedges shield the finely groomed space from passersby.

I turn my head toward the delicate white gazebo and I stare, my mouth dropping open and my body temperature rising. He's here. My behemoth sits on a bench, the wooden slats bending under his tremendous weight, his shoes planted solidly on the ground. He has set his coffee cup beside him and is frowning down at a tablet, his shoulders slightly hunched over.

No one should appear so sad and alone, especially not a magnificent man like him. Before I realize what I'm doing, I move toward his bench, seeking to be closer to him, to comfort him.

My stranger glances upward as I approach and his gaze claims mine, his eyes as black as his suit, his countenance hard and unyielding, unmistakably dominant. I tremble with sexual appreciation. He's even more impressive up close and I want to crawl onto his lap, put my arms around his neck, and press his face between my breasts. Instead, I sit on the bench directly across from him, place my brightly colored tote beside me, and cradle my cup of coffee between my palms.

He tracks my movements silently, his lips lifting slightly. He doesn't speak. He doesn't move. He merely watches me, gazing at me as though I'm the center of his universe.

I like that he gives me his full attention. I like it very much.

"Hi," I murmur, my voice breezy and my chest tight. "I saw you in the coffee shop." This sounds as though I'm stalking him, so I hastily add, "I didn't follow you. I spotted the park this morning and thought it looked like a nice place to drink coffee. Though I shouldn't have coffee because I'm really strung out as it is."

He narrows his eyes, his thick eyebrows lowering.

"Because of jet lag," I explain. "Not because I'm on drugs. Drugs are bad. Gotta keep it real." My laugh is shaky. "I'm messing this up, aren't I?"

"No." His voice reaches down deep inside me and curls around my heart. As I wait for him to say more, I sip my coffee, the whipped cream tickling my nose. He gazes at me. Silence stretches between us.

Silence reminds me of death. "Good," I chirp, clinging to my newfound happiness. "I didn't want to scare you away from your park. This place is beautiful, isn't it?"

I glance around us. Happy yellow, white, and blue flowers add lines of color between the green hedges and the grass. Beads of dew glisten on the delicate petals. A floral scent floats on the morning breeze. The two of us are seated steps away from the busy street and sidewalks, yet we're hidden, secluded and alone in our secret space.

"It *is* beautiful." My behemoth toys with his tablet and I glimpse flashes of silver. His palms are lined with thick deep scars. Someone has hurt him badly and he must have spent days, weeks, maybe months, lying in a sterile white hospital bed recovering. Did a loved one sit by his side, talk to him about silly things like fashion and shoes, the inane chatter making him smile?

"This weather is seductive." I set my cup of coffee on the bench and lean my head back, enjoying the warmth of the sun's rays on my skin. "I don't know how people can bear to wear clothes on days like today." I unbutton the top button of my blazer.

He blinks slowly, his eyelashes obscenely thick. "You're wearing clothes."

"I'm pale and I burn." I undo another fabric-covered button and his gaze lowers to my chest. "And I don't want you to get the wrong impression about me." I arch my back, the pose lifting my breasts.

His lips curl upward. "And what impression is that?" He's sexy and strong and I want him more than I've ever wanted any other man. There's nothing stopping me from having him. Here, in LA, I have no obligations, no duties to perform, no expected image to project. I can be happy and free.

"You'll think I'm not a nice girl." My voice grows

husky. "You'll think I'm naughty." I slip the third button through the hole and spread the fabric open.

"Are you naughty?" His dark eyes gleam.

"I could be." I've spent the past five years ruthlessly controlling my reckless streak, being responsible, careful not to cause my father more anguish and stress. But my father isn't here and he won't ever hear of this encounter.

I wiggle my toes, too excited to remain still. "I could open my blazer, allow you to see me. Would you like that?" I ask my behemoth, hoping he'll say yes and make one of my secret fantasies a reality.

He pauses for a heart-stopping moment and then inclines his head.

"Okay." This encounter should scare, not stimulate me. He's a stranger, a man I don't know. We're outside. Anyone can enter the park and see me. My fingers shake as I undo the fourth button. "You can only look. You can't touch, understand?"

"I understand." He leans forward, his gaze stimulatingly intense. Although I trust him to keep his word, I'm also aware that rescue is only a scream away.

"I've never done this before," I confess, releasing a fifth button. "Yes, I might have flashed some teenage boys at a pep rally back in high school."

I hesitate. That confession isn't the complete truth. My senior year at high school was when I *started* exposing my body to strangers, the fast, thrilling spurts of rebellion taking my mind off more serious matters I couldn't control. The adrenaline high hooked me, my exhibitionism quickly progressing from a temporary escape to a sexual need, a need I wouldn't hide from my behemoth.

I decide to be completely honest with him. "More recently I flashed a man or two or four on the subway, but that was a quick lift of my blouse as the train rushed past. I doubt they saw anything."

My stranger's shoulders shake. He's laughing at me. I narrow my eyes at him and he stills.

"This is different." I undo the final button and my blazer falls open, revealing my lavender lace bra. My breasts are large, filling the cups, my taut nipples visible through the thin material.

His gaze remains fixed on my face. "This is very different," he agrees, his muscles coiling, the tension stretching between us palpable. He wants me and he's strong enough to take whatever, whomever he wants. But he won't move and he won't hurt me. I know this in my soul.

"You can look at me." I give him permission, needing his gaze on my body.

He peruses me slowly, silently, and I bask in his attention, in the appreciation of this man I don't know. He could be anyone—an off-duty policeman, a university professor, my new boss. All of these possibilities excite me.

"Touch yourself." His voice rasps across my skin, the sound more stimulating than any caress.

I obey him without thought, without hesitation, cupping my curves and lifting them, offering my body to this stranger in the park. My passion rises as I squeeze and release my breasts.

I press my knees together, struggling to control my excitement. This is wrong, so very wrong. I lower my gaze to his lap, seeking reassurance that I'm not alone in my desire, that I'm not the only person aroused. My stranger is hard, his cock jutting against his black dress pants, his erection as large as the rest of him. I lick my bottom lip.

"Show me your pretty pink nipples," he demands, pushing me further than I've ever gone. I look along the path, scared and excited, my body ready to combust. We're alone, the park deserted except for the two of us. "I'll protect you," he assures me. "No one else will see."

He's right. My blazer shields my naked skin. Only this man seated directly in front of me can see my breasts. I pull my bra cups down, brazenly freeing my nipples.

He growls softly, the primitive sound of his approval urging me onward. I pinch and pull my sensitive flesh, the sweet pain shooting directly to my pussy. I'm wet, my panties soaked, and I'm needy, so very needy.

Does he want to touch me, to fasten his lips around my nipples and suck on my breasts? I imagine the tug and pull of his mouth on my skin, the firmness of his big hands against my ass as we grind together, seeking sexual satisfaction. I wiggle on the park bench.

"What do you like, kitten?"

My father calls me Kit Kat. Other people call me Kat, short for Katalina. I meet my behemoth's gaze. "I like it when you call me kitten." I know this isn't what he's asking.

He smiles, his straight white teeth flashing in his tanned face. "Do you like having your breasts played with?"

I shouldn't be having this conversation with a stranger. "Yes." I bow my spine, pushing my breasts into my palms, fantasizing he's the one holding me, touching me. It has been so long since I've been touched by a man.

"That's it, kitten," he coaxes. "Play with your breasts for me." I knead my curves, wishing to please him, to please myself. "Do you like having them kissed?" he asks.

"Yes." I picture his face buried between my breasts, his golden tan contrasting with my pale skin. His mouth will be hot and wet, his suction unrelenting, pain mixing with my pleasure. I pant, working my breasts harder, rubbing my pussy against the bench, the friction escalating my desire.

"Do you like having them fucked?" His low voice adds to the sensory assault.

"Ummm . . ." I've never considered this option before. I lower my gaze. His pants are tented around his hard cock. What would it feel like to have his shaft cradled between my breasts? I run my tongue over my lips. "Yes?"

"Close your eyes," he instructs and I comply, trusting him. The darkness heightens the brush of my fingers over my breasts, the grind of my pussy against the hard wooden slats. I moan softly, swiveling my hips.

"Imagine I'm straddling your chest," he rumbles. "Do you feel the weight of me? The warmth of my skin?" I nod, trembling. I'm close, so close. "My big cock slides between your breasts in and out, in and out. I squeeze you around me. My hands are rough and scarred."

"Yes, please." I rock, ravishing my breasts with my hands, tugging, squeezing, twisting my nipples. My curves are bared to this stranger, to anyone who enters the park. Only a hedge separates us from the bustling city streets. I'm exposed, vulnerable and completely his, trusting him to keep me safe.

"You do please me." His words flow over me, adding fuel to my flames. "My balls are aching and I want to come over your beautiful white breasts, over your pink nipples." The tremors rolling up my body grow more and more powerful, my arms and legs shaking. "But I can't come until you do, kitten. Tell me what you need from me to get you there."

"Smack my clit." I breathe heavily.

"Yes." His approval warms me. "Reach under your pretty purple skirt and smack your clit for me. Smack it hard." I hesitate. This is wrong. We're in a public park. "You need this," he adds.

He's right. I need this release. My emotions are too close to the surface, too unmanageable. Once I come, I'll feel calmer, more able to cope with my eight o'clock appointment.

"Okay." I sigh my surrender and slide my right hand under my skirt, between my thighs. My desire builds, escalating higher, my body stretching tight.

I position my hand over my mons and slap the heel of my hand against my clit. The pain breaks me, shards of pleasure shooting over my body, color and light bursting against the darkness of my closed eyelids. I bite down on my bottom lip, silencing my screams, and arch and buck and writhe, shameless in my satisfaction.

Gradually I return to reality and to the realization of what I've done. I'm sitting in a public park with my skirt hiked up and my blazer open, my face flushed with ec-stasy. *He* sees me like this. I avoid my stranger's gaze as I pull down my skirt, adjust my bra, and button my blazer, my movements sharp.

"You're beautiful, kitten," he says softly.

He must think I'm completely uninhibited, a woman without any morals. "I've never—"

"I know you haven't done this before." He raises one of his big hands, stopping my explanation. There's no judgment in his dark eyes, only an understanding. "Why did you choose this morning? Why here? Why with me?"

"I don't know," I answer truthfully. A combination of factors might have contributed to my insanity—the stress of the new job, the sadness haunting me, and him, the most magnificent man I had ever seen. "I trust you."

His eyes harden and his jaw juts. "You shouldn't trust me. You don't know me. If I had been someone else—"

"If you had been someone else, I wouldn't have done this." I bend down and wipe the dust off the toes of my lavender pumps. "Don't you feel the connection between us?" I cover up my insecurities with a smile.

My sexy stranger sighs. "Yes." He slides his tablet into his inside jacket pocket, stands, tosses the coffee cup in the garbage can, and takes three steps forward. He's even larger upright, his form over a full foot taller than mine. "I'm walking you to the office."

I check my watch and my eyes widen. "It's five min-utes to eight." I jump to my feet, my cute heels crunching on the gravel. "I'll be late for my first day at work." I place my coffee cup beside his in the garbage can and sling my tote over my shoulder.

"Are you nervous?" The stranger walks beside me, matching my shorter stride.

"Of course I'm nervous." I slide one of my hands into his and his fingers close around mine, his palm grooved with deep furrows. "I'm a new intern and interns are chosen by their executives. What if no one chooses me?"

"You'll be chosen." My behemoth's grip on my hand intensifies. He smells of lemon and cedar. Not a hint of cigarette smoke spoils this pussy-moistening combination.

"I left the experience section of the application blank." I chew on the inside of my cheek. "I helped my father, but I didn't know if that counted as experience and I didn't want to lie." I lied about my last name. I didn't want to lie about anything else. "My father always tells me business deals are built on trust and trust is built on truth."

My stranger turns his head and meets my gaze, his forehead furrowed with thought lines. "Your father always tells you that?"

I nod.

There's a long pause in our conversation, as though he's giving my father's words deep consideration. "He's right," my mystery man finally concedes, his voice gruff.

I beam at him, liking him even more for agreeing with my father. "Will I see you tomorrow?" I want to see him, very much.

"Yes," he rumbles. I wait for him to say more. He doesn't. He slows and then stops. "I'll leave you here." He reluctantly releases my hand, his fingers slowly sliding along mine, his scarred skin rough.

I tear my gaze away from his, stare up at the building belonging to Blaine Technologies, and frown. "How did you know this is where I'm working?"

He doesn't answer. I glance to my right. He's gone, his distinctive scent lingering on the morning breeze. I breathe deeply, inhaling that part of him, square my shoulders and stride into the building.

About the Author

Cynthia Sax lives in a world filled with magic and romance. Although her heroes may not always say, "I love you," they will do anything for the women they adore. They live passionately. They play hard. They love the same women forever.

Cynthia has loved the same wonderful man forever. Her supportive hubby offers himself up to the joys and pains of research, while they travel the world together, meeting fascinating people and finding inspiration in exotic places such as Istanbul, Bali, and Chicago.

Please visit her on the web at www.CynthiaSax.com

Visit www.AuthorTracker.com for exclusive information on your favorite HarperCollins authors.